Rats!

"Uncle, what is it?" Quangster whispered.

"Nothing," Hercules answered quickly. But his heart froze as he finished reading the words in silence:

I, UKBAT, CLAIM THE THRONE OF RATS. I HAVE SLAUGHTERED THE MICE AND TAKEN THEIR SKULLS FOR MY SCEPTER. MAY MY REIGN BE AS LONG AND BLOODY AS MY FATHER'S. MAY MY SONS KNOW THE GLORY OF BATTLE AND THE SWEET TASTE OF MOUSE BLOOD UNTIL THAT GLORIOUS DAY WHEN WE HAVE DESTROYED EVERY MOUSE FROM WITHIN THE WALLS. LONG LIVE THE EMPIRE OF RATS AND UKBAT ITS KING!

For a long moment, Hercules looked at the words and at the hideous iron decorations on the Box. He thought of his mice sleeping so happily under the new cheese-sun, and he looked at Quangster, so faithful and trusting. . . . and at that moment, he vowed that he, Hercules Amsterdam, would save them all.

"[Readers] will find Hercules and his fellow adventurers to be interesting, multifaceted characters with a very unusual story to tell. Try this on dedicated fantasy fans."

—*School Library Journal*

OTHER BOOKS YOU MAY ENJOY

THE HEROIC ADVENTURE OF

HERCULES AMSTERDAM

Melissa Glenn Haber

PUFFIN BOOKS

PUFFIN BOOKS
Published by Penguin Group
Penguin Young Readers Group,
345 Hudson Street, New York, New York 10014, U.S.A.
Penguin Books Ltd, 80 Strand, London WC2R ORL, England
Penguin Books Australia Ltd, 250 Camberwell Road, Camberwell, Victoria 3124, Australia
Penguin Books Canada Ltd, 10 Alcorn Avenue, Toronto, Ontario, Canada M4V 3B2
Penguin Group (NZ), cnr Airborne and Rosedale Roads, Albany, Auckland 1310, New Zealand

First published in the United States of America by Dutton Children's Books,
a division of Penguin Young Readers Group, 2003
Published by Puffin Books, a division of Penguin Young Readers Group, 2004

3 5 7 9 10 8 6 4 2

THE LIBRARY OF CONGRESS HAS CATALOGED THE DUTTON EDITION AS FOLLOWS:
Haber, Melissa Glenn.
Hercules Amsterdam / by Melissa Glenn Haber.
p.   cm.
Summary: A human boy, just three inches tall, finds a home and happiness
in a mouse city until he learns of an ancient threat and goes on a
dangerous quest to save the city, assisted by old friends and new.
ISBN: 0-525-47119-7 (hc)
[1. Size—Fiction. 2. Mice—Fiction. 3. Individuality—Fiction.
4. Advneture and adventurers—Fiction.] I. Title.
PZ7.H1142He 2003
[Fic]—dc21 2002040808

Puffin Books ISBN 0-14-240216-8

Designed by Heather Wood
Printed in the United States of America

ACKNOWLEDGMENTS — First and always, thanks to Ezra Glenn, best friend, husband, and best of fathers; to my four parents and all my in-laws; to my sister, Deborah; my sons, Linus and Tobit, and my daughter, Mehitabel; to Mattie and to Jeremy Astesano for all the names; to Aine Farrell; to Anna Guillemin for friendship and the providential sequence of e-mails she set in motion; and above all to my exceptional editor at Dutton, Jennifer Mattson, not only for changing my life, but for being the best teacher of writing I've ever had. Thank you.

THIS IS DEDICATED TO

THE ONE I LOVE, EZRA

AND ALSO TO

ALEX NICELY JOHNSON,
FOR WHOM IT WAS ORIGINALLY WRITTEN

THE HEROIC ADVENTURE OF

HERCULES
AMSTERDAM

HERCULES AMSTERDAM WAS only three inches tall, though no one knew exactly why. There were many competing theories. His father thought he didn't get enough exercise. His grandfather thought he didn't drink enough milk. His grandmother blamed Hercules' mother for smoking too many cigarettes while she was pregnant, but Hercules' mother blamed Hercules. She thought that he could be as tall as other children, if only he wanted to.

Whatever the reason, by the time he was nine years old, Hercules was not much taller than a mouse would be if it stood on its hind legs. You can understand how this made things difficult for his family. Even the simple things of life—breakfast, for example—were complicated by the difficulty of using eyedroppers to serve up his soft-boiled eggs or finding tweezers to tease apart a grapefruit so he could eat it. And though Hercules had rigged himself up a little table and a tiny chair so he could sit on the tabletop next to his father's plate, he was in constant danger of being knocked over by elbows and cereal boxes and coffee cups, and, if he tried to venture across the table to serve himself from the common dish, the lazy Susan in the middle might suddenly twist under his weight, and he would go sprawling, dazed and dizzy, into somebody's oatmeal.

There was also the problem of the cat. She had lived with Hercules' parents long before he was born and showed no signs of leaving. When Hercules complained for the hundredth time that the cat would eat him for lunch, his mother finally lost her patience.

"Don't be ridiculous—she's always taken care of you like you were one of her own kittens. Cats—don't—eat—people. Don't be so scared of everything."

Hercules glowered at her insensitivity. He wanted to explain that it was easy to be scared when you were only three inches tall, but he knew she wouldn't understand. Eventually they came to a compromise that the cat would not be allowed into his room, which his mother thought more than settled the matter. Hercules wasn't so sure. He had never seen the cat signal her agreement to the bargain.

On the grounds that it was absurd to expect someone only three inches tall to attend school, Hercules had always refused to go, and taught himself out of the books his mother brought home from the library. Though it was exhausting to stand on the floor beside the open book and use both hands to turn the pages, he read for hours each day. He was convinced he had learned much more than he would have from teachers. His mother always argued that school would make him happy, but Hercules disagreed. He *was* happy, he insisted. He *liked* the comfortable solitude that came from being only three inches tall.

An added benefit of his height was that he had a whole house to himself—not just a bedroom, like other children, but a whole Victorian dollhouse that had once belonged to his mother. It was very elegant. The living room had a bay window with real glass panes that looked out on his little garden of plastic perennials. Two large bookshelves framed the window, and though it was not actually possible to remove the books and read them, they gave a cultured look to the room. There was also a working rolltop desk and even a grand piano.

A beaded curtain hung between the living room and the kitchen. In a fit of ingenuity, Hercules had made it out of twelve beaded light-pulls, and he often enjoyed walking through the curtain, feeling the strands of beads falling around him. Otherwise he had little reason to go into the kitchen—its wooden appliances were pretty much only ornamental. The bathroom, too, was mostly for show. Although it featured real porcelain fixtures—a sink, tub, and toilet—none of them had running water, which, you'll agree, is somewhat essential in such items. Of course, people who lived in real Victorian homes in real Victorian times did not have running water either, so Hercules did as the Victorians had done—he had someone fill up the tub with hot water from another tap, and he used a chamber pot instead of a toilet. The chamber pot was like a porcelain potty that had to be emptied into the toilet by someone else, usually his mother—Hercules suspected this was one of the main reasons she wanted him to grow. The chamber pot was a very interesting item. It was bright white, with a pattern of blue flowers around the outside, and on the inside it was decorated with blue letters that read: *Keep me neat and keep me clean, and I won't say what I have seen.*

The bathroom led to a hallway that was home to an inexplicably large collection of souvenir pencils. They stayed there because that was where Hercules' mother had always kept them when she was a girl, and Hercules had never had a reason to move them unless he had need of stilts or tepee poles or the like. Past the pencils was his bedroom: Hercules always gazed at it with pride. Although its elegance was somewhat compromised by the wood-patterned Con-Tact paper his mother had installed on the floor, the room was very comfortable. It had a four-poster brass bed, covered with sheets made from a real silk handkerchief. A skylight let in the sunshine that came in through the windows above his dollhouse.

All in all, Hercules explained to his disbelieving parents, he was satisfied with his dollhouse, his books, and his life. When they were not there to see him, however, he spent long hours sitting on top of the bookshelf beside the dollhouse, looking out the windows to the world outside. Outside was so beautiful, so tempting, but above all, so dangerous! Whenever his parents convinced him to take a walk with them, his chest tightened as soon as they opened the apartment door. The sprawling Victorian house in which the Amsterdam family lived had been converted into two apartments, but it kept its ornate, sweeping staircase that climbed dizzying heights to the second floor. When Hercules stood at the top of that precipitous flight of stairs, he could barely stand the vertigo. The only thing that made it worse was his parents' cheerful obliviousness. "Come on!" his father would coax. "There's nothing like a walk to relax the mind!"

Relax! It was a joke. When he actually made it down the terrifying stairs and out the door, there was always the danger of bicycles and skateboards and Rollerblades. Though it had never happened, he lived in mortal terror of being brained by a falling acorn, and viewed the autumn as a season of extreme peril. And then there were the bees—bees that were to Hercules the size of immense buzzing dogs that chased him screaming from the flower beds. And dog-sized *bees* were nothing compared to dog-sized *dogs*. Even the small arthritic Yorkies that lived in the downstairs apartment could have killed him with a little nip of their yapping mouths, but they were not the worst: there were also the neighborhood Dobermans and Rottweilers and German shepherds who could easily swallow him whole and still need some other tidbit to round out the meal. No, there was nothing to relax the mind outside. It was only back in his room that he breathed easily, lolling on a good book or writing with a mechanical-pencil lead wrapped with masking tape to strengthen it. Then the sounds of outside—the barking of dogs and the occasional screeching of hawks, the sound of wheels on the asphalt, the squawking of the neighborhood children—all these faded into the distance, and his room was so quiet he could hear the squeaking of mice in the walls.

One day, as he was tacking up one of his drawings onto the back wall of the living room, he discovered that the squeaking in the bedroom wall behind the dollhouse was particularly loud. It made him smile to imagine that there might be a family of mice living inside the walls of his parents' house, just on the other side of where his dollhouse touched his bedroom wall. He had always known there were mice in the walls of the house, of course—it was the reason his mother had first gotten the cat—but this was the first time he had stood still to listen. He was surprised to find that the cadences of the squeaking were much like human speech. Now and again (perhaps because of his small ears, or the fact that he had heard the squeaking all his life), he discovered that he could understand a phrase of it, as clear as English, and the words all seemed to squeak of family, of friendship, and of love.

He began to look forward to hearing the mice. He re-arranged the furniture in his house to make eavesdropping more comfortable, moving the bed, piano bench, and chamber pot to the back of the dollhouse. He spent hours with his ear pressed up against the dollhouse walls, listening and learning the mouse language. Some nights, as he fell asleep to the sweet sound of a mouse mother squeaking a lullaby to her young, he remem-bered the way his own mother had sung to him as she rocked his cradle. In those times he felt a great longing to hear all the words of the mouse's song.

It wasn't that he didn't love his own parents; it was simply that they had never really understood what it was like to be only three inches tall. He knew they loved him, but it would have taken a less perceptive boy than Hercules to know that the two of them would have been a lot happier if he'd been more like other children. His father had always wanted a son to chuck the old pigskin around with, a son to take to baseball games; but with Hercules, he had to be content with unsatisfying games of catch using a Ping-Pong ball. Whenever they played together, his father would reminisce about his own childhood and the long hours he had spent playing baseball with his friends, and then he would sigh nostalgically and say he knew Hercules would have liked it, too. Once, trying to be kind, Hercules suggested that they go to the baseball diamond and at least roll the old pigskin around, but his father had responded morosely that the pigskin was a football, not a baseball, and that he guessed it wouldn't really work, anyway.

Hercules agreed with relief. He remembered the one Little League game they had gone to together, and tried to imagine himself standing in the orange clay beside home plate, choking on the dust. He imagined the cleated feet of the other players narrowly missing him as he ran the interminable distance from base to base, and he thought about the flying baseball that could crush him like a meteor falling from space. Then (thinking of these dangers and not of the game of catch) he missed his father's warning and took a Ping-Pong ball to the face. He spent the rest of the afternoon lying down with a kernel of frozen corn on his nose, to keep it from swelling.

It was not much better with his mother. She simply refused to believe that Hercules would not be happier going to school and making friends. Hercules didn't bother to explain that children could be even worse than baseballs and dog-sized bees. He had seen it with his own eyes. There were three boys who lived on his street and Hercules often watched their exploits, how they threw rocks at birds, and pulled the wings off flies, and said horrible things to other children in the neighborhood.

One day in May, shortly after his tenth birthday, his mother appeared in his room. Hercules had spent the morning wrestling with several dozen of the superfluous souvenir pencils, lashing them together to make a ladder. He was just climbing up the ladder to the top of his bookshelf to look out the window to the street outside when he noticed her across the room, crouching down and peering into the dollhouse to see if he was there.

"I'm here," he shouted, and she looked up and blinked.

"Hi, honey," she said, coming over to the bookshelf and examining the ladder closely. She studiously avoided meeting his eyes; it was not a good sign. It meant bad news was coming.

"Hercules, honey, I'm thinking of going back to work."

Hercules waited.

"So I think it's time we talked about going to school."

There it was. No matter how many times they had this argument, it always filled Hercules with alarm. How could he go to school? It was impossible to imagine how he would climb to the top of a mountainous desk, let alone lift the slab of a textbook with him—plus the crush of feet, plus dodgeball—and besides, where would he go to the bathroom? Mutely, miserably, he shook his head.

His mother fished a piece of nicotine gum from her pocket and began to chew it nervously.

"I can just stay here while you're working," Hercules suggested.

"Oh, Hercules," his mother sighed, "you're too young to stay here alone."

Hercules said nothing; he had learned to win this argument with silence. His mother sighed again and leaned over to rumple his hair with the tip of her finger.

"We'll talk about it later," she said, and then she left.

Hercules sat at the window for a long time, pressing his face against the screen. He bit at his nails. He had not told his mother all the reasons he didn't want to go to school. Right outside were three of them now: the three boys who lived on his block. They were using a turbo squirt gun to spray water into the open windows of the neighbors' houses. Hercules' heart froze. *His* window was open, too. The boys advanced; the gun moved ever closer to his window. Hercules panicked. He lost his footing and fell behind the bookshelf.

There wasn't much space between the bookshelf and the wall, and Hercules scraped against both all the way down, skinning his arms and legs. He lay still a long painful moment after he landed, gingerly feeling his limbs and staring up at the strip of sky and the deep festoons of ropy dust above him. It was a long time before he saw the hole in the baseboard. When he did notice it, he felt certain it was the path to the kindly mice he had been listening to for so many months. Cautiously, carefully, hopefully, he poked his head inside.

"Hello?" he called.

His call echoed in the darkness: the mouse hole seemed empty. He ducked inside the hole and then back out again, but the darkness and the strangeness were too much for him. And perhaps there was another fear behind it—a fear that if the mice were not what he hoped, he would be truly alone. He climbed out from behind the bookshelf without exploring more, but from that moment on, whenever he thought about school, he remembered the little hole and felt better.

Several days passed before his mother mentioned school again. But one morning, when he was accompanying her on her errands, she suddenly veered off her expected course and walked up to the elementary school around the corner. She didn't even stay on the safe side of the fence, as she usually did when they strolled past, but headed straight into the fray. Hercules cowered miserably in her pocket. He kicked at her side to signal that they should leave.

But after a moment, his curiosity got the better of him, and he cautiously poked his head out and looked around. It was not as bad as he had expected. He watched the kids playing four-square, and they all seemed very good-natured; he watched the bouncing braids of the girls as they performed the complicated step-step-step of double-Dutch jump rope, and it all seemed very friendly. Even the sounds were comforting—the chatter around them blended together like the courting of a thousand crickets. Hercules felt himself relaxing for a moment. He noticed a chubby, untidy girl sitting against the fence, reading one of his favorite books. For a moment, he wished he could talk to the girl and ask her what other books she liked. He was just poking his mother to ask her to move closer when he saw how the other kids made wide circles around the girl as they walked by.

Hercules winced, and then the whole school yard snapped into focus. It was not all good-natured. Not six feet away he could see a skinny-necked boy choking back tears after ricocheting between two sets of unfriendly elbows. Hercules quailed; he imagined what those malicious elbows could do to him, he who was even smaller than a clenched fist. He could not help but see the kids who came reluctantly off the bus and looked up at the school with a sigh. He stared in appalled sympathy at the children whose hats were jerked from their heads and tossed from hand to hand, always out of reach. He kicked at his mother, to tell her he wanted to leave; he wanted to be safe at home, curled up on the pages of a good book.

But his mother was oblivious to the nastiness and cruelty all around them. She strode up to the reading girl and asked her if she knew the way to the office.

The girl looked up and blinked behind her glasses before answering.

"I am in fact intimately acquainted with its location," she replied wryly. She folded down the corner of her page and placed the book in her knapsack before scrambling awkwardly to her feet. Hercules breathed a sigh of relief; she had not noticed him at all. He shrunk farther into his mother's pocket, amongst the keys and loose change and sticks of gum, and kicked his feet frantically. But Hercules' mother seemed too interested in talking to their guide to notice.

"Are you thinking of sending a child here?" the strange girl inquired briskly as she led them into the school. Hercules peeked out again, taking in the grimy halls and flickering fluorescent lights. "Well, I wish I could give you a better report of this particular institution of learning. It certainly leaves some things to be desired on the educational front, let me tell you. And I should tell you in the spirit of full disclosure that many of its inmates are somewhat less than civilized. Oh, pardon me— I have been reprimanded several times for using the term *inmates*. Ah, well. But here we are, the office." She bowed formally and smiled. The smile helped ease some of Hercules' anxiety, and he was just wishing that she would stay and talk a little longer when the bell rang. The girl saluted Hercules' mother, squared her heavy knapsack on her shoulders, and walked away.

Hercules' mother nodded absently and turned to the receptionist. She was so busy asking questions that she never noticed Hercules slipping from her pocket. Grabbing the cord to the venetian blinds, he hauled himself up to the ledge of the window that looked out onto the corridor. He parted two slats of the closed blinds and peered through the chicken-wired glass.

The girl was strutting up the hall away from him, her overloaded knapsack swaying heavily as she walked. Before she disappeared out of view, he saw two tall boys step forward and accost her. They were huge boys—they towered over the pudgy girl like rats crouching over a mouse. From the looks of it, they were saying terrible, teasing things to her, and though her patient face did not seem disturbed, it made Hercules suddenly want to cry. Behind him, his mother was asking worrisome questions: "I know the school year's almost over, but what about summer school? And what about facilities for children . . . uh . . . with special challenges?" Hercules barely heard her. He pressed his face closer to the glass and saw one of the boys reach out and shove the girl against the wall, knocking her glasses askew.

With that, Hercules had seen enough. Without knowing what he was going to do, he slid down the cord and dropped the last two inches to a chair below. He slid to the floor down the chair's leg and (racing along the walls so as not to be stepped on) ran until he found the open front door. A moment later, he was halfway across the school yard. He scurried down the sidewalk and around the corner to his own street, hauling himself over the oak roots that had grown through the pavement in front of his house. He stood for a moment in front of his door, gasping for breath. There was a small package waiting on the front steps; Hercules shoved it closer to the door. Then, with a creak and a squeak, he was through the mail slot and into the front hall. The staircase up to his second-floor apartment had never looked so daunting, but Hercules didn't care. Climbing the netting that his mother had nailed between the banister and the stairs so he couldn't tumble off, he reached the top of the landing and squeezed under the door to his apartment. He stood panting for a moment in the hallway, looking toward his room and considering. Then he raced toward the kitchen to the little insulated bag where his parents kept his snacks and grabbed a piece of cheese as large as his head. In a fraction of a moment, he was down the hall and in his room. He took up a drawing he had done of some mice and scribbled a note on the back telling his parents not to look for him and not to worry. A second later, had anyone been watching, they would have seen Hercules Amsterdam disappearing behind his bookcase.

IT WAS VERY DARK INSIDE the mouse hole. As Hercules crept forward, the little archway of light that was the entrance grew dimmer and dimmer in the distance, like a tiny flame flickering out. Before long it was impossible to see. He crept along, one hand touching the dusty side of the passage, and walked smack into a wall in front of him. *This must be the corner of my house,* he reasoned, rubbing his nose. *The passage must be heading into the wall behind my dollhouse.* Cautiously, keeping one outstretched arm before him, he followed the passage as it turned to the right. There, in the darkness ahead, he saw a dim glow that grew brighter and brighter, like a tiny spark catching flame. Suddenly the path ended; a little ladder led down between two joists into the brightness below. Hercules climbed down and gasped.

Instead of the emptiness he had expected between the inside and outside walls of his house, he was standing on a ledge above an impossibly long and narrow cavern. A great ball of fire was suspended before him. It flamed like the sun, though this sun seemed to burn in a bronze basin, hung by wires from the cavern's ceiling. Quite unlike the sun Hercules knew outside, it appeared to give off the strong odor of feet, or perhaps a very old and stinky cheese.

He stood there in awe. He was looking over a city, but it was like no city he had ever imagined. Innumerable terraces had been built along both sides of the cavern, with ladders and steep switchbacking paths connecting one level to the next. Dozens of brightly painted houses perched on each terrace, while little bridges no wider than a wire connected one side of the city to the other. Down at the bottom of the great cavern, which Hercules assumed must be the floor of the downstairs neighbor's apartment, a city square sparkled under the malodorous sun. A huge fountain spouted there, ringed by great public buildings with wide pillars and golden domes. To Hercules' eye, the most wonderful sight was the busy activity: mice playing by the fountain, mice hanging out their laundry, mice fearlessly crossing the narrow wire bridges high above the city square.

Hercules looked around him, trying to get his bearings. A wide expanse opened up beside him, and he guessed he was looking into the space between the first-story ceiling and the second-story floor. Peering into it, he was astonished to see what seemed to be gardens and, behind those, a little baseball diamond complete with bleachers. Hercules smiled to think that the little clicks and clacks he had always heard coming from the floorboards might have been balls hitting the ceiling as the mice scored home runs. He inched toward the field. Three mice were throwing a ball back and forth next to the pitcher's mound, all standing on their hind legs, as proper mice do when no people are looking. Cautiously, Hercules moved toward them.

"Hello," he said tentatively. He was surprised (though perhaps not as surprised as he might have been) to hear that his words came out in mouse-squeak.

"Hello," the mice replied one by one, a little bit dubiously. In the long and uncomfortable silence that followed, Hercules had the growing impression that they were too polite to comment on how strange it was to have a human, however small, suddenly appear in their midst.

"Why did you come here?" one finally blurted out. The others seemed shocked at his boldness.

Hercules considered this for a moment. "I was lonely," he said finally. There was another pause; the mice apparently did not know the word. "I brought you some cheese," he added.

"That's an odd present," said one mouse. "Or do you want to give it to our parents?"

"I thought mice *liked* cheese," Hercules said, feeling defensive.

"It's a very nice present," the smallest of the mice said kindly. "Maybe our mother will let us have a cheese lamp in our room at night."

"Why don't you just eat it?" suggested Hercules unhappily. "Here—*I'll* eat some. Look . . ." And he took a nibble.

"Oh, don't waste it!" the smallest mouse cried. "We didn't mean to act as if we didn't want it!" Quickly she took up the cheese in her little paws and nimbly ran with it across the bridge to the other side of the cavern. Hercules stared. She moved as easily as a tightrope walker in the circus. A moment later she returned with a large lantern. It was burning with a soft flame and gave off a pleasant light. "See," she soothed, "we love it. Normally we reserve Swiss for special occasions—not that this isn't a special occasion, of course."

"Monterey Jack gives off the best light, *I* think," one of the others interrupted. "It's so festive."

"I bet *you* like cream cheese, eh, Sangster?" the third teased his sister. "That lavender light—so *romantic*." Hercules stared. Then he raised his eyes to look up at the burning sun on the ceiling of the cavern. It occurred to him he had a lot to learn about mice. But then again, he was not planning on going home—there was all the time in the world to learn.

"Can I see the rest of the city?" he asked eagerly.

The mouse called Sangster exchanged glances with her brothers. "Can't you see it?" she asked, peering down at the city square and the houses that rose up on both sides of the cavern. "It's right there."

"No, no," Hercules said. "I mean, will you show me around? I've never been within the walls and I'd like to see how mice live."

"All right," she replied, "but it's just our city, and we just live here."

Happily, Hercules followed the mice down sloping paths and ladders through the mouse city, always refusing to cross the terrifyingly narrow bridges. The city was delightful. The tightness that usually squeezed his heart when he was among others was gone. The mouse city was serene. There were no cars, no blaring music, no barking dogs, but quite a lot of squeaking, especially in the city square, where the large fountain was surrounded by dozens of mouse children and young mice courting. Young fathers and mothers promenaded around the fountain, pushing huge carriages filled with six or more pink and hairless babies, and glowing under the compliments of passersby. There were numerous open-air cafés where mice sat eating plates of roasted seeds and drinking flavored water, and there were little carts that sold mice cream. Sangster bought some for Hercules. It was sweet and delectable, served in a cone that he could hold in a single hand. Everything was just the right size for him, and it was glorious. For the first time in his life, he swung on a swing. He slid down a slide. He rode the merry-go-round; he rode it a hundred times. He drank lemonade. He sighed with contentment. The mouse world, he felt, could not have been more perfect had he invented it himself.

"What else can we see?" he asked Sangster. "What else do tourists do here?"

"Tourists?" she repeated.

"I mean, what do other mice do when they come to visit?"

"I don't know what you mean. We visit each other, of course, but we are all already here."

"You mean this is the only mouse city within the walls?"

"This is the world," she answered simply.

"But where do you think *I* came from?"

"I don't know," she said. "I haven't considered it." She ducked her head, then, and refused to answer any more questions. When Gangster and Fangster appeared a moment later to see if Hercules wanted to come see their collection of comics, she seemed greatly relieved.

Hercules went and admired the comics, although he couldn't read the swirling tailscript in which they were written. Gangster and Fangster couldn't read it either, but they spent the afternoon laughing at pictures of mice triumphing over the clumsy, dim-witted rats and the sly, self-centered cats. By the time Sangster and her brothers laid dinner on the table, it was understood that Hercules would be staying the night. Sangster's parents didn't seemed to mind. They hardly seemed to notice that he spent the next night, too, and the next, and the next, and the next. By the end of the week, everyone acted as if he had been staying there all along, and it was tacitly settled that he could live with them as long as he liked.

His circle of acquaintance grew daily, and none of the mice seemed to think it strange that a very small human had come into their lands. In fact, they never referred to his humanness at all. Sangster, especially, seemed to consider it rude to acknowledge that he was anything but a mouse.

"Why do you wear clothing, even when it's not a festival day?" Fangster asked once.

Hercules looked from his shirt and pants to the naked fur of the mice and tried to explain about human modesty. But Sangster, as if embarrassed by the subject, shushed him.

"Maybe it's because every day is a kind of festival day, now that you're here," she said, giving Fangster a severe look.

Of course there were times that he felt like a stranger in a strange land. At first, for example, they did not know what to call him. None of the mice could pronounce his name, because mice can't make the same sounds as humans. Finally they gave up. "What does it mean?" they asked him. "Maybe we can say it in mouse-squeak."

Hercules drew himself up proudly. "Hercules was a great hero, a strong man and a brave one," he told them.

"But you are just a child," they said.

"True," he admitted.

"We will call you Too-Small-for-Name," Fangster suggested. "But what about your other name, the one that sounds like our word for a disease of the tail?"

"Amsterdam," Hercules answered, "is a great watery city far away."

"Like the sewer pipe where the rats live in the comics?" Sangster ventured, because she always tried to understand Hercules' strange ways. For a long time after that, they called him Too-Small-for-Name Sewer-Pipe, but after they got to know him better, they gave him affectionate nicknames—Small Ears, Fur-on-Head, and No-Tail. And he was very happy.

"Mice are always so kind," he said once to Sangster.

She looked at him quizzically. "Kind?" she repeated.

"Kind, you know—thoughtful. No one tries to be mean. . . ."

"Of course not, life is too short," she responded.

"Where I come from—" Hercules began, thinking of the school yard, but Sangster suddenly changed the subject as she always did when he spoke of the world outside the walls.

"Come on!" she called brightly, heading back to the city square. "Let's try again to get you across the bridge."

"I don't think I can do it," Hercules objected. He looked up at the bridges that spanned that chasm. It still made him dizzy to see the mice scurrying across them, and his one attempt on the very lowest had ended badly in the most undignified rescue. It was, if nothing else, a reminder that some things are always frightening, even if they are your size. "I *can't* do it, Sangster. I don't think my feet are made the right way. . . ."

"Sure they are," Sangster called over her shoulder. "*Every*-mouse can do it, Small Ears!"

And though Hercules never could bring himself to use the bridges as a shortcut, it didn't matter. Sangster was always willing to go the long way around with him. And as they followed the winding switchback trails down to the city square and back up the other side of the cavern, they would meet other mouse children who would invite them to go swimming or play a game of baseball.

Fangster and Gangster always thought it hysterical that Hercules claimed humans had invented baseball. It was the favorite pastime of mouse children and the occupation of many a long afternoon. The mice quickly accepted Hercules into the game and, for the first time in his life, he was a natural. He was by far the best pitcher the mice had ever seen because of his flexible human shoulders. And so he went from not being able to play any human sports at all to being a baseball star, which was all right by him.

Mouse baseball was the same game he had watched at home with his father, with a few exceptions that Hercules chalked up to the relatively short attention spans of the mice. For example, the first was that the game was automatically over if any team scored three runs, and it never went longer than three innings. Similarly, there were only three balls before a walk, and once, when Hercules was pitching a little wildly and was sure that he could throw a strike the next time, he demanded that they use human rules and allow four balls. "We always play by *your* rules," he complained. "Why can't we just play my way for this one time—" He stopped, because the mice were looking at him blankly.

"It's not that different," he wheedled, "just four balls instead of three. . . ." Then he stopped, too. When he had said the word *four*, he had used the English word. He found that he did not know the mouse word for *four* at all or, for that matter, any number higher than three.

"What did you say?" they asked, baffled.

"Four," he said again in English. "Four. Four. Four."

They shook their heads in confusion.

"One, two, three," he counted, in mouse-speak, and then, in English, "four, five, six. . . ."

After several moments of looking at Hercules as if he were a madman, Sangster turned to a mouse beside her. "Do you think he means *lak*, Bangster?" she asked. Bangster shrugged.

"*Lak?*" Hercules asked. "What's *lak*?"

Sangster timidly waved her paw at the mice beside her. "One," she said, pointing to Gangster. "Two," she said, pointing to Fangster. "Three," she said, pointing to Bangster. *Lak*," she said, pointing to the rest of them.

Hercules stared. "Are you telling me none of you can count higher than three?" he asked. He suddenly felt a touch of superiority and it was very satisfying.

"Sure we can," said Sangster, offended. "One, two, three, *lak*." All the mice nodded, as if it were Hercules who didn't understand.

Hercules drew some sunflower seeds out of his pocket. "Are you telling me," he repeated, "that you don't see any difference between *this*"—he dropped four seeds on the ground—"and *this*?" And he dropped five beside the pile of four. The mice shook their heads. "What about *this*?" he asked, dropping the whole lot of them.

"That's *lak lak*, of course," said Fangster dismissively. "Every blind and hairless mouse baby knows *that*."

But Sangster, after some mental struggle, understood what Hercules was trying to say. "Do you mean you *know* that number?" she asked, staring at him in amazement.

"That's just a handful," Hercules said impatiently. "But that's not the point—"

"What does it matter?" appeased Fangster. He was looking greedily at the *lak lak* pile. "Who needs to know? We know *lak*, we know *lak lak*, and no mouse has ever needed to know different. Let's get back to the game."

But some of the other mice couldn't quite let it go. Fairly often they would recall the time that Hercules had tried to cheat at baseball by invoking some strange counting game. They stopped calling him Small Ears or Fur-on-Head or No-Tail or any of the other old names and called him He-Who-Counts-Past-*Lak*, which they meant as a teasing kind of name. Hercules didn't care. He chose to take it as a compliment.

3

AND SO THE MONTHS PASSED, and Hercules was very happy. Outside the walls, the days grew longer and then shorter again. But inside it was always the same—the comics, baseball, mice cream. Since mice children did not go to school—except a few like Bangster, who had wanted to learn enough to read the comics—they had plenty of time to play. They built a tree house in a stand of copper water pipes. They went boating in an immense pond that had once been formed when the water pipes had frozen and burst. They climbed the broken wires that hung down like vines at the lake's shore and swung out over the water. They put on plays. They took a tent and camped out in the baseball diamond. They stayed up all night telling stories, which was easy to do because there was no night or day between the walls, where the cheese-sun burned brightly at all hours.

Of all the mice, Hercules was fondest of Sangster, who had always tried to understand him. One day, while they sat in the tree house cracking seeds between their teeth and Hercules was trying for the *lak lak*th time to explain about human ways and human houses, he finally threw up his hands in defeat.

"Why don't I just show you?" he said. "Come with me and you can see for yourself where I used to live."

Sangster looked away. She blushed so hard Hercules could see it through her brown fur.

"I know you don't really understand our ways yet, Small Ears," she scolded him gently, "but it's not in the best of taste to talk about Outside the Walls."

Hercules stared at her. "Why?" he asked eventually.

Sangster looked uncomfortable and suddenly pointed to the nearest bridge. "Would you like to try the bridges again, Small Ears?" she asked. "I think you'll get the hang of it if you just re-member not to look down. Let's go now and—"

"*Please* come with me," Hercules begged. "Isn't it rude to refuse a heartfelt invitation, especially from a friend? Where I come from, it is."

Sangster hesitated miserably, torn between the demands of competing etiquettes. "All right," she gave in at last, "let's go."

She grew visibly more nervous as they climbed the ladder to the corridor to the mouse hole and clung to his arm as the passage grew dark. When the mouse hole began to glimmer in the distance, she gave a little squeak. As they came through the opening and into Hercules' room, the squeak died in her throat and she stared in mute amazement at the sun—the real sun—that was beginning to stream through the windows. She blinked, and stared, and then her voice came back in a rush.

"Your sun is so much brighter than ours!" she exclaimed. She pranced about the room, poking her twitching nose into every corner. She was very impressed with Hercules' dollhouse and squealed with pleasure when he played the piano. Proudly he showed her the real glass in the bay window and let her play with the top of the rolltop desk. Then he remembered the garden. Telling her to look upstairs by herself, he slipped out the dollhouse's back door.

He was just bending over to select one of the plastic flowers for his friend, when he heard a panicked shriek followed by a yowling that sent his heart to his mouth. The cat! That horrible cat was in his room! He ran back inside. The open side of the dollhouse was now blocked by fur and claws and whiskers. The cat had Sangster cornered in the hallway. Hercules sprang up the stairs. Sangster was throwing the superfluous souvenir pencils at the cat's face and shrieking each time she missed. In a moment Hercules was at her side. Using his flexible human shoulders, he launched a pencil into the air like a javelin and struck the cat full on the nose. She let out a wail and ran from the room. Hercules turned to comfort Sangster. She was huddled in the corner, looking quite small.

"Take me *home*," she demanded.

Hercules found that he was still clutching the plastic flower in his left hand. Embarrassed, he let it drop behind him and escorted her toward the mouse hole. He found he was opening and shutting his mouth stupidly, unable to think of anything to say.

As they approached the mouse city, however, Sangster began to chatter happily about the pleasant things she had seen, and Hercules began to swell with pride at the memory of his valor. But when they came to the baseball diamond, she ran from his side to Bangster's and began talking very quickly without referring to their adventure—not even once mentioning the cat. That night after dinner, when Sangster had still neglected to mention that her life had been in mortal danger (or the small fact that Hercules had rescued her from death), he began to feel a tiny bit impatient for his glory. He did not want to toot his own horn, of course, but he thought he might hand it to Sangster and have her toot it for him.

"Tell them about the cat," he said, a little more unsubtly than he'd intended.

Sangster gave him a shocked look, as if he'd been unspeakably rude.

"He-Who-Counts-Past-*Lak* made up a story about a cat," she mumbled to Bangster. "It was very funny."

Hercules began to object, but Sangster gave him a stern look as if she were his mother and he held his tongue. Later that evening when she caught him alone, she whispered, "I know you don't understand all our ways yet, Small Ears, but it is really considered rude among us to mention some subjects."

"It's rude to talk about cats?"

"It's *more* than rude," she answered firmly. "Mice never speak of cats or . . . never mind. Let's just not talk about it."

"But Sangster . . ." Hercules started. "Don't you want them to know what you really saw?"

For the first time since he'd known her, Sangster grew snappish and angry. "Oraclees," she said, mangling his name as she did in moments of great seriousness, "if you're going to be a mouse, you have to learn to live like a mouse." And she never would talk about the cat again.

One day in July, when Hercules had been living with Sangster's family for two months, Bangster surprised him by suggesting Hercules take a little house of his own. Hercules did not know Bangster well—he had always felt Bangster was a little stuffy, always trying to seem more grown-up than he was—and he didn't know how to react.

"Why?" he asked finally, trying to keep the suspicion out of his voice.

"It would keep you from feeling that you're a burden to Sangster's family," Bangster explained, in a voice that suddenly made Hercules feel awkwardly underfoot.

"I've found a suitable residence for you," Bangster went on stuffily. "It's a little one-room cottage up on one of the highest levels, perfect for a bachelor such as yourself."

Hercules hesitated, but Sangster eagerly agreed to visit the new house with him. When she saw it, she took his arm and pressed it enthusiastically.

"Oh, it's lovely, Small Ears," she exclaimed. "Just look at the view! And really, houses on this side of the city are very desirable—it's much warmer in the winter. And besides, we're just across the way."

Hercules looked dizzily down into the city square, and out across the narrow chasm to Sangster's home.

"It will take me an awfully long time to get over to you," he said. "I'll have to go all the way down to the city square and then all the way back up the other side. . . ."

"You'll just have learn to cross the bridges," she replied, and to show him how easy it was, she tripped lightly over the wire strung over the cavern and disappeared into her own house. That night she returned with Bangster and a newly filled cheese lamp. "Mozzarella, that's for hospitality," she quoted. Hercules started to respond, but Sangster had already turned away. "You did a wonderful job choosing a house, Bangster," she said softly. "I look forward to the house you'll choose for *me*." Then she walked quickly around the little room, throwing open the doors and windows to greet Hercules' friends. They came with roasted seeds and with sugar cakes to welcome Hercules to his new home and, as is traditional with mouse housewarmings, they kept him awake the whole night reading comics and singing humorous songs.

Hercules came to love his new house. He was certain that he would be happy living in the mouse city with Sangster and her brothers forever. But mice grow up much faster than boys and girls do, and it wasn't long before Hercules found that fewer and fewer of his friends had the time or the inclination to play three innings of baseball with him. First Gangster and then Fangster drifted away from the daily game and then, one day, Sangster was nowhere to be seen. Hercules searched all around the city, storing up funny and interesting things he wanted to tell her. She was not by the lake or the fountain or any of the other usual spots, but late in the afternoon, he heard her clear laughter coming from the hydroponic gardens. There he found her with her head on Bangster's lap. Bangster looked up with aggravation, but it was the barely hidden look of annoyance on Sangster's face that made Hercules stammer his apologies and leave.

Not many weeks later, much to Hercules' surprise, he was invited to a string of weddings, and then (not three months after he first came within the walls) Sangster was showing off the first of her litters of blind and hairless babies, with Bangster standing proudly at her side. Though they asked him to be godfather, Hercules felt with sadness and confusion that the happiest chapter of his life was ending. He still visited Sangster nearly every day, but their conversations were always interrupted by the needs of her scampering babies, and often they did not say three consecutive words to each other. It did not get better. By the fall, Hercules' little godsons and goddaughters were marrying and having children and grandchildren of their own, and Sangster was a sedate matron who had no time left for Hercules at all.

The next few months were difficult. Hercules found it exhausting to have to make a whole generation of new friends every few months and began to spend more and more time by himself. Some days, as he sat alone in his little house, he heard the muffled sound of a television coming from the other side of the wall. At those times, he thought of his parents and the rest of the world outside and wondered if he should go back. But then he would listen to the television announcer read the terrible news of the day and, remembering what he had seen in the school yard, he dismissed the thought from his mind.

He took instead to exploring every inch of the mouse city. One day, when he was feeling particularly dark and moody, he decided to follow one of the passageways that disappeared into the blackness. With a lantern and a substantial snack of a raisin in his knapsack, he headed away from the soft glow of the cheese-sun. His brooding thoughts kept him company as he walked along the switchback trails, and soon he was lost. Darkness had completely befuddled his sense of direction, and he had no idea how long he had been walking. He did not know if he had walked around one side of the house or three; he didn't know if he had climbed up three stories or none.

All of a sudden, he was swept by a nauseating panic. For a moment, it seemed possible that he might be lost forever in the labyrinth of empty passages that crisscrossed through the walls of his house. In the eerie silence, broken occasionally by creaks, his breathing seemed so loud that it must have belonged to some other animal, perhaps one lying there in wait.

Taking a deep breath, Hercules marshaled his courage and lifted the cheese lantern higher to examine his surroundings. There, on the wall, was an inscription written in the mouse language. He stared at the delicate, incomprehensible swirls of tailscript with relief. He must have walked all around the four walls of the house and come back home to the mouse city. Eagerly, he went forward, expecting at any moment to see the blaze of the cheese-sun. But there was no flare of cheerful light. There was only the glow of his own lantern, which fell not on dusty trails, but on the shapes of buildings. He *had* made it back home, but all was dead and quiet. Hercules looked skyward. Hanging from the cavern's high, vaulted ceiling was the bronze chandelier. It was empty now and hung crookedly from two of its chains. A cold terror crept up from his knees.

"Sangster!" he cried out. "Gangster! Fangster!" But there was no answer, not even an echo. The city was desolate. There was no sign of his friends.

It was impossible that it was the mouse city, he thought anxiously, but (he had to admit) how could it not be? Everything was the same—here was the fountain, surrounded by the cafés where Sangster had first introduced him to mice cream. It was clearly the same fountain, with all its carvings of mice at play, but it was dry, and the graceful spouts and spigots had all been smashed as if with furious hands. His heart beat frantically as he climbed one of the broad roads that led upward to the baseball field. It was so familiar that he hardly needed his little lantern to find his way. There were the bleachers, standing empty in the darkness. From the edge of the baseball field, he looked down over the city. There was the cheese-gatherers' hall, with its golden roof caved in; across the way was Sangster's house, with all its windows broken; there was his own little cottage, its door swaying on broken hinges like a loose tooth. There were no signs of life at all.

It couldn't be the city where he'd been happy these past few months, he thought desperately. It was much too smothered with dust—it was practically choked with it. With the hairs prickling on the back of his neck, he walked back down to the town center. The dust stood in great heaps here, heaps as tall as dunes on a beach. Hercules bent down to touch it. It was not dust—it was ash.

There had been a fire.

There had been a fire and the whole mouse city had burned. But when? The ash was cold, he felt with relief—it was only the memory of a fire that had raged long ago. When did it happen? Was this one of the electrical fires he had once heard his parents talking about? It *must* have happened long ago, but still—just to be certain—he thought he should go back and make sure his own city was safe. He raced back the length of the passage without stopping once to catch his breath.

When he came back to his own city, he stood for a thankful moment, looking up at the pure white light of the cheese-sun, shining brightly in the sky. His eyes lingered on the buildings, whole and clean. He smiled down on a whole unfamiliar passel of young mice who were playing around the tinkling fountain, eating their mice cream. But still, he felt nervous. He ran until he found Sangster. She was sitting in her kitchen, busily knitting pair after pair of little booties for her sixteenth set of great-grandchildren. The way the light fell on her face made her look very old.

She did not stop knitting for a moment while he was telling her his story, and when he was done she held up one finger as a signal to wait while she fixed a dropped stitch. Then she looked up at him with motherly patience.

"Have Gangster and Fangster been telling you ghost stories again?" she asked. "You're old enough not to trust them—even if you don't look it," she added indulgently. "Everymouse knows those old stories, but they're just stories. My grandmother's grandmother and her grandmother's grandmother have lived here all their lives, and no one's ever seen the ghost cities. It's all stories to frighten children with." She resumed her knitting.

Hercules did not know what to say.

"Is it possible that you are getting bored here, Small Ears?" she asked gently, careful not to look at him. "I suppose it must sometimes get boring for you, now that all your friends have . . . other concerns. You are of course welcome among us for as long as you need us, but perhaps it is time you thought about returning to your own world with the beautiful sun and the cunning little rolltop desk—do you ever think of that?"

"I'm not bored," he cut in. "And I have plenty of new friends."

"Of course you do," she said. She bound off the knitting and bit through the yarn with her sharp little teeth. "Come back and cheer up an old lady again soon, Small Ears."

He tried to be mouselike and put the image of the burned

city out of his mind, but he could not stop thinking about the eerie desolation—the violent destruction of the beautiful fountain, the creaking of the broken chains. He began looking for someone he could tell, but though he did have many acquaintances among the mice, all of them quickly remembered other engagements when Hercules started to describe the ruins.

The only one who listened was Quangster, one of Gangster's great-great-grandchildren. He was a very small mouse—the runt of the litter—and Hercules had always felt very protective of him. He liked Quangster's quiet earnestness and his eager curiosity: he was the only mouse who had ever asked Hercules about the world he had come from, though he always acted as if Hercules were making it all up.

"Really, Uncle? They fly around in the sky and eat peanuts? You should write for the comics. You have the best imagination in the whole world, I think."

It was more or less the same when Hercules described the destroyed city. Quangster listened attentively and even pressed for more detail, but when Hercules begged him to come along and see it, even Quangster grew agitated, and claimed to believe it was only a story. He was clearly terrified to believe it was more than that. After all, he was a very young mouse, even younger than Sangster had been when Hercules had first met her.

One day, when Hercules was at home working on a map of the world within the walls, Quangster knocked shyly on his door.

"What are you doing, Uncle? Is that a map?"

"Yes—of that city I told you about."

Quangster smiled. "I've been making up a story, too, Uncle! I've brought it here so you can see it." And proudly, nervously, he showed Hercules a comic he had drawn himself, all about a giant mouse who went to live with humans. The pictures were very crudely done, and his ideas of the world outside the walls made Hercules smile.

"I could show you the real world outside the walls," he offered.

But Quangster blushed from his whiskers to the tip of his tail and choked, "No, thank you, my uncle." With an awkward bow, he snatched up his papers and dashed away.

Hercules might have been content to leave Quangster in his ignorance had he not made a second venture into the walls. This time, as he walked on the dark and forgotten paths hours from his terraced city, he came across a strange, smooth tunnel. Unlike the paths of mice, which traced natural features like beams and pipes, this one plowed right through the wooden joists of the house. Following it, he came to another mouse city—silent, dead, and destroyed. He bent down and examined the jumbled footprints on the ground and—here and there among the running marks of mice—he found larger prints, with claws, that made his skin crawl. It suddenly seemed like a very bad idea to be exploring all alone in the creaking darkness, having nothing to defend himself with beyond some seeds and a bottle of water in his knapsack. He hurried back to the mouse city.

Back under the cheerful light of the mouse sun, everyone was too busy with children or work or baseball to accompany Hercules in search of mythical cities. Hercules sighed with exasperation. He was left with only one choice.

"Quangster," Hercules said, when he finally located his young friend near the cheese-gatherers' hall, "I need you to come with me. Please! I need someone—I need *you*—to see what I've found."

Quangster nibbled on his claws and his tail quivered. He looked up at Hercules with pleading eyes. He hesitated a moment and then shook his head mournfully.

"Please," Hercules begged.

"All right," sighed Quangster. "For *you*, my uncle." And he reluctantly followed Hercules out of the city.

Quangster grew more and more uneasy as the mouse city disappeared in the distance. It was not too long before he began to pretend he thought that Hercules was taking him on a wild-goose chase. At least Hercules assumed he was only pretending, because he couldn't help noticing how fast Quangster's nose was twitching or how his whiskers stood all on end. Quangster began to walk slower and slower. It seemed to take an immense effort on his part to put one paw in front of the other. Finally he stopped in his tracks. "I can't go farther, Uncle," he said timidly. "I—I must get back to my duties at the cheese-gatherers' hall—"

"Please come with me, Quangster," Hercules implored. "Someone else needs to see this."

"I'm so sorry it can't be me," Quangster whispered, and then he was gone. Morosely, Hercules continued on, marking his route on the map.

It was not too long before he stumbled on a ruin he had never seen before. This one proved to be the most mysterious of all. All the buildings in the city square had been completely destroyed except one towering brick wall that had once been the back of the cheese-gatherers' hall. Now it stood like an ominous billboard, covered with inscriptions in big, thick, aggressive tail strokes. The very sight of the immense letters made Hercules' heart pound in his chest. They were ugly and menac-

ing and chilled him to the bone. He kicked himself for not having used his weeks of loneliness to learn how to read tailscript.
I'll just have to find someone to read it, he said to himself, and he
turned over his map and began to copy down the strange letters
with shaking hands. When he was done, he looked from the paper to the wall to the bleak desolation around him, and then,
with a shudder, he hurried back home to the mouse city.

BACK IN THE MOUSE CITY, it proved remarkably difficult to find anyone who could tell him what the tall writing said. Neither Gangster nor Fangster nor Sangster could read, and Bangster could just barely sound out the words in the comics. None of them knew anyone else who could help.

Finally, Hercules grew exasperated. "How can a whole city be full of illiterates?" he snapped to Fangster.

"Who needs to read?" Fangster replied. "I mean, the comics are fun, but Bangster can tell us what they say. There are enough mice who know how to read."

"*Everyone* should know how to read," stated Hercules emphatically.

"Why?" soothed Fangster. "Does everyone know how to build houses, or make mice cream, or light the cheese lamps? A society works best when you divide up the labor. My job is to care for the babies, Gangster works in the gardens, and your job—your job is to be *interesting* to the rest of us."

"But whose job is it to know how to read books?" asked Hercules, not sure if he should be pleased or insulted to be called *interesting*.

"Well, of course, there's the Steward of the Chronicle, who reads us our history every Sun-Day, and there's the Librarian for everything else," said Fangster.

"There's a library here?" Hercules asked. "I've never seen it."

"Of course we have a library," Fangster said, clearly offended by Hercules' surprise. "It's out at the edge of town, near the dump."

"Of course," sighed Hercules.

Following Fangster's directions, he walked along one of the upward-sloping boulevards for several levels until it turned into a broad avenue, past the baseball fields and gardens and the big public ovens and then into a small street, and finally into a little neglected pathway that led past the dump. Beside it was a tall, cylindrical building, somewhat like a smokestack. The doors creaked and moaned when Hercules pushed them open.

He entered into a great foyer with a dusty black-and-white marble floor, all lit by a massive, ornate cheese chandelier suspended from the ceiling, two stories above. The walls were lined with what looked like wooden honeycomb, but when Hercules approached, his heels echoing on the marble floor, he realized that each of the thousands of holes was filled with a roll of paper. Tentatively, he pulled one out. Unrolled, it was nearly as wide as his outstretched arms, and covered with delicate tailscript.

Hercules rerolled the scroll and was about to push it gently back into the hole when a voice came from above and startled his heart into his throat.

"May I help you?"

For a long moment he could not locate the owner of the voice. He turned around in a circle, but the room was empty. Finally, he looked upward and saw that an octagonal balcony ran around the edge of the round walls. Closer inspection revealed that a spiral staircase, hidden behind honeycombed panels, wound up to the second level.

A massive desk blocked his way at the top of the stairs. A mouse was seated behind it, staring down at Hercules like a judge. He held his blackened tail in his paws as if he had just been writing.

"May I help you?" he asked again in a disinterested voice.

Hercules took the paper out of his pocket and slid it over to the mouse. "Please," he said, "I was looking for someone who could tell me what this says. I copied it down and no one else can read it."

Disdainfully, the mouse reached over and examined the paper. He folded it negligently and handed it back to Hercules. "It says nothing," he said. "It is nonsense. Gibberish. They aren't words at all. You must have copied it wrong. Where did you find it?"

With a sinking heart, Hercules recited his story.

The mouse clicked his tongue impatiently. "I haven't time for this nonsense," he interrupted. "Go round yourself up some youngsters. They always like a good ghost story—even if they've heard it before." He looked at the scribbled map on the other side of the paper and snorted. "Now, I've given you all the time I have. You've interrupted me just as I was finishing this chapter, and I need to get it all down before I lose the inspiration."

"Why won't anyone believe me?" Hercules blurted out. "I was there! I saw those buildings! Why doesn't anyone want to know what happened?" His voice echoed around the walls of the great room, sounding peevish and small.

But the mouse behind the desk had stopped listening. He had begun to write again, moving his tail with rapid movements across the paper spread out on his desk. He did not look at Hercules again.

As if to break the awkward silence, the door downstairs creaked open. The Librarian peered over the edge of the balcony and sighed in annoyance. *"Olfer,"* he groaned, and began to write in a frenzy. In a moment, the oldest and slowest mouse Hercules had ever seen came creeping up the stairs. As he drew near, Hercules could see that his eyes were covered with a strange white film.

"Etchel, are you here?" the old mouse called.

With an aggravated look and an exaggerated sigh, the mouse behind the desk finished the word he was writing and threw down his tail with annoyance. "Yes, Grandfather," he groaned.

The old mouse ignored Etchel's irritable tone and spoke in an even voice. "I have come again to ask you to reconsider my request, my grandson," he said.

"I have reconsidered it many times," Etchel replied, "but as I have always concluded, I don't have the time. I have my writing to consider. Of course, it is a great honor, but I—"

"It is not for your honor that I ask you," the old mouse countered, "but for the honor of all mice. Since this city was founded, *lak lak* suns before your grandmother's grandmother's grandmother, it has always had a Steward to record our history and keep the Chronicles of the Stewards who have come before. Our Chronicle is the core of who we are. It has been preserved through every disaster. But when the sun burns out and the next is lit, who will write the new entry, if I have no Little Steward? I cannot see to do it. And when I die—for I will die soon, Etchel—who will follow in my footsteps? Who will have learned the secrets of the Steward? Are our records to stop now because no one will take up the responsibility? What will we be then, Etchel, with no history?"

"Grandfather," sighed Etchel, "I would if I could, but my duties. . . ." His eyes flickered back to the scroll on his desk. He looked itchy with impatience to get back to it. Then he caught sight of Hercules.

"Grandfather," Etchel said, with more animation than he had shown before, "there is a . . . *youngster* here full of questions about our history. He has come here looking for answers."

The old mouse turned toward Hercules. "Is that your breathing I hear, my grandson?" he asked.

Hercules stepped forward and took the old mouse's wrinkled paw. "I would be honored if you would talk to me, Grandfather," he said.

The old mouse held Hercules' hand for a moment. "Your paw is unusual, and your voice is strange," he said, "but if your heart is willing. . . . Come with me and let me hear your questions. Then we shall see what we shall see. Etchel, please open my office."

With another sigh of impatience, the Librarian stepped from his desk. Hercules followed as Etchel led them to a room at the top of another winding staircase. The iron shutters that lined the walls within were tightly shut, but the room was suffused with a soft green light. When Hercules looked up, he saw that the roof was carved from a large green stone—an emerald, perhaps, or possibly a beer bottle. Etchel led the old mouse to a chair and sat him down, and then hurried out of the room. Hercules could hear him clattering down the stairs.

"Come and sit, my grandson," the old mouse said to Hercules in his calm voice. "I am Olfer the Steward. Who are you?"

"My name is Hercules Amsterdam, Grandfather," he said.

"I have never heard such a strange name, my grandson," the old mouse said. "But you have questions about our history?"

"Grandfather," said Hercules, "I have seen what no one believes that I have seen and I have found writing that no one believes can be read. It troubles me, my grandfather."

"Alas," the old mouse said, "I wish I could decipher it for you, my grandson, but as you can see, I am blind." He settled himself on his chair. "Still," he went on, "I am not yet deaf. I will listen to what you have to say."

Once more Hercules recounted his trips between the walls. He told the old mouse about the destroyed and abandoned cities he had seen; he told him of the great wall of menacing writing. Olfer listened gravely, his face very close to Hercules, as if willing his blind eyes to see. When the story was done, he took Hercules' hand again and held it for a long time as he seemed to consider his next words. Then, with a small nod, he began.

"I am the oldest mouse in this city," he said slowly, "and even I have never met anyone who remembered anyone who remembered being in those other cities. Those stories have come down to us only as myth. But perhaps they were once true, once, *lak lak* generations ago."

"Then you believe me?"

"I believe you," Olfer replied slowly. "I am old, as I have said, and I have learned that there are more things between the walls than are dreamed of in your comics."

"How old *are* you?" asked Hercules, gazing at the old mouse's grizzled muzzle and at his strange whitened eyes.

"I have lived for three suns," the old mouse said. "Three times I have seen the sunlamp burn out and be relit. If I see it one more time, I will have lived longer than any other mouse in our history. No mouse has ever seen the sun relit *lak* times."

"May you see it relit *lak lak* times," said Hercules earnestly. "Grandfather, there is much I do not know. Perhaps you can explain it to me. How long does each cheese-sun burn?"

"A mouse born when the sun is new will see her grandchildren's grandchildren before the next sun is lit," the old mouse replied, and Hercules calculated from his experience that a mouse sun was little more than a human year. "It is a very long time," Olfer went on. "And according to our history, it has been *lak lak* suns since this city was built after the last one was destroyed."

"So you *do* know about those other cities, Grandfather!"

"Yes," said the old mouse, "but, my grandson, most mice believe they are only myths. Most consider it rude to say that they are true, to suggest that we live in a world that is less than perfect."

"But the world is not perfect," said Hercules fervently. "I know it isn't. I have seen it."

"Yes," said the old mouse, "I believe that you have. And I understand you want to know the truth. In this, you may be alone. Mice today want to be entertained by the comics. They do not care about the real stories. But I hear in your voice that you are different. Is it true you desire to hear our history, to know who you are?"

"Yes," said Hercules, "I want to know who I am more than anything else."

The old mouse stood up painfully and walked over to the shelves behind him and, feeling with his arthritic paws, groped among the scrolls until he found one wrapped in soft leather. He opened the scroll with the loving pride of an artist showing his work. It was covered with the beautiful swirling tailscript of the mice.

"Ever since Ulrich came out from the woods and found the first cavern between the walls," the old mouse began in a singsong voice, "we mice have kept this Chronicle under the guardianship of a Steward. We have added to it at each relighting of the sun to tell of our doings since the last sun was lit."

"What does it say?" breathed Hercules.

"Have patience, my grandson," said the old mouse. "Our civilization is now at a crossroads. I have no Little Steward, no one to help me keep our records and be Steward after me, for I have outlived all my successors. I can find no one new who will be my student. Etchel will not. He was my last hope. But perhaps *you*, my grandson, are the right mouse to follow me. Are you established? Is your family able to be without you for many hours in the day?"

"I don't see much of my family," admitted Hercules guiltily.

"Are they all grown? What is the size of your family? How many great-great-grandchildren do you have now?"

"I don't even have children yet," said Hercules, thinking about his parents. He wondered if they had taken his tiny chair off the dining-room table yet, or if they looked at it with sadness as they ate their dinner. He swallowed hard.

"You are younger than I believed," said the old mouse, as if to himself. "I never thought a mouse could be so young and yet so interested in our past. But let us work together, my grandson. We will see if it is your fate to be the next Steward of the Chronicle."

"But, Grandfather," admitted Hercules, "I cannot read the tail writing."

"Of course not, my grandson," said the old mouse kindly. "So few mice learn to read even the comics these days. But I will teach you as I was taught all those suns ago."

He put his paws on the unrolled scroll that lay before them on the table. "Do you see the tail writing, how it is broken into different shapes? Each shape represents a sound in our language. Look at the first sentence, down in the right-hand corner. The words run from right to left from the bottom of the page up. Do you understand?"

"Yes," said Hercules, "but it does seem a little backwards to me."

"It is always confusing in the beginning, my grandson, but before the next sun, I am sure you will understand. Now look at that first sentence again. This is what it says, 'Behind the tail of Ulrich the Leader we have left the woods.' The first word is *behind*. Do you see it? Each shape represents the sounds in the word *behind*. Here is ink. Dip your tail in it and copy down those sounds."

Obediently Hercules dipped his finger in the ink and tried to approximate the swirling shape of the symbols, writing the English letters that each one represented beside it.

"The second sentence reads, 'We have founded a city. Let it grow for *lak lak* suns,'" recited the old mouse. Again, Hercules wrote down the new letters. By the third sentence, he had learned all twenty letters of the mouse alphabet, and slowly, like somebody translating a code, he began to read out loud to the old mouse. Occasionally he made a mistake, reading from left to right, and once from top to bottom, but the old mouse was pleased with his progress and praised his skill. Hercules blushed with the pleasure of Olfer's approval. Later, in his little house, Hercules tried out his new skill. Taking out the map with the ominous writing on the back, he tried to translate the tail strokes, carefully starting at the bottom right and working up to the upper left. After a few minutes, he had to admit Etchel had been right—the words were gibberish. In frustration he thrust the paper back into his pocket and went out to find comics for practice.

By the following week, Hercules had undoubtedly mastered reading tailscript. Proudly he read out loud to Olfer: "'It is dark in the city. The sun does not rise. The mice cry out for a little light. Ulrich the Leader has gone to search for a new sun.'"

The old mouse stared at Hercules reprovingly.

"You have tricked an old mouse, my grandson," he said, and Hercules began to fear that Olfer had figured out that he was human. "You knew how to read all along."

"No, my grandfather," Hercules said quickly. "I'm just good at this kind of thing." He read on. "'Ulrich the Leader has returned. In his journeys within the walls, he has learned a magic. He has taught us that mice may no longer eat cheese. Orcster the Six-Toed Metal-Maker made him a lamp. He signed his name in gold. Ulrich placed the cheese in the lamp and lit it with the magic. It hangs above the city like a sun, a sun with a delicious smell.'"

The old mouse looked at Hercules in astonishment. "No mouse has ever learned to read so quickly," he said. Slowly he reached out and touched Hercules' arm. For a moment his paw lay still and tense on Hercules' skin. Then he relaxed. "All right, my grandson," he said. "I believe you. It may be that you are special. If so, perhaps it was meant to be that you should become the next Little Steward."

SO HERCULES WAS NAMED Little Steward of the Chronicle.
It was not a moment too soon, for even to Hercules it was obvious that the sun was dying. The city swirled in a frenzy of
preparation for the relighting. All the streets were washed free
of dust and the fronts of the buildings were repainted. The water in the fountains was dyed different colors and the tailors
worked long hours making festival clothing. While the others
prepared, Hercules stayed cloistered in the Steward's chambers
in a panic. Writing the new entry in the Chronicle would be his
first official act. He practiced frantically for hours every day.

He felt the lack of a tail keenly. Mice write in huge, sweeping motions, and Hercules' writing did not have the free abandon of the great mouse calligraphers; in fact, it looked a little as
if a ten-year-old boy had tried to copy John Hancock's signa-

ture at the bottom of the Declaration of Independence. He practiced into the small hours of the night, as the cheese-sun outside grew dimmer and dimmer. Each day he stared at the sun, trying to gauge how much longer it would burn. Finally one day, when he had just decided that he would never be able to produce an acceptable approximation of tailscript, there was a sudden sputtering from outside the window and then darkness. The sun had burned out.

By the time he reached the town square, it was as busy as a hive. All the mice knew just what to do. In the dim light of cheese lamps and lanterns, they shimmied into their new clothes. Several mice raced to the city center, lowered the great bronze basin that held the sun, and began to polish it. From closets and cellars, the older mice brought out long poles from which they hung their lanterns, and everyone congregated under the swinging lights near the stage that had been built in front of the cheese-gatherers' hall. There was the excited murmur of expectation from every corner, and the lanterns swinging on their poles lit up the happy faces of every mouse present.

Although Olfer had told him exactly what would happen at the relighting, Hercules was unsure of himself. He looked around for some familiar face and with relief saw Sangster surrounded by dozens of great-grandchildren and great-great-grandchildren. She smiled as she took him by the hand. "Happy Sun-Day, Small Ears," she said sweetly. "They're waiting for you, up on the stage." Hercules felt faint. He looked up at the stage and saw Olfer standing beside Ghin, the mayor, and Dounster, the head of the cheese-gatherers' guild. The old mouse held the Chronicle in his crooked paws, standing as still and as dignified as a statue. Hercules swallowed once and pushed his way through the crowd to join them on the stage.

"The sun has burned down to nothing," the mayor intoned, and Hercules felt sure that these words had been spoken many times before for countless generations. "Today we light it again, in the same lamp Orcster the Six-Toed Metal-Maker signed his name to, using the same magic Ulrich the Leader found between the walls."

Olfer edged forward. He seemed very small and crooked, but his voice was so sweet and sure that it almost made Hercules want to cry. "At each relighting of the sun," Hercules heard him say, "the Stewards have always read our Chronicle and added a new entry. Attend and listen!"

Olfer spoke. He spoke, and spoke, and spoke, reciting the words from the Chronicle. Hercules watched the crowd. Although it was hard to see in the dim light of the lanterns, he was certain not everyone was paying attention. As the history of the generations went on, he noticed that the crowd appeared to be thinning; soon he realized it was because so many had lain down to sleep. He was glad that Olfer was blind.

"Thus is our history written," the old mouse boomed, and *lak lak* mice and one human jumped. "Now it is time for the new entry to be included in our Chronicle. Let the Little Steward step forward."

Nervously, Hercules advanced and accepted the bottle of ink the mayor handed to him. Olfer began to speak in his clear, confident voice. Hercules scrambled to write down his words, hardly knowing what he wrote.

"Thus a new chapter is entered," the old mouse concluded, and Hercules had to stop himself from writing those words as well. A lackluster cheer came up from here and there in the crowd. Hercules checked over his writing, wincing at the ugly letters that lurched across the page. As he read, he was first surprised and then indignant. The entry was all about the election of Ghin as mayor and the repair of the town-hall steeple. It made no mention of the arrival of a small human to the city within the walls.

He looked out into the crowd. Of the few who were paying attention, none seemed to think it odd that the entry transcribed by a small human did not mention that small human at all—none of the mice seemed to care. Instead they were watching Ghin expectantly as she cried, "Now, as Ulrich the Leader taught us, let us have a sun once more!" To the fanfare of squeaking trumpets, four young mice came forward, struggling under an immense load of cheese. Hercules saw Quangster among them and tried to catch his eye. A few of the cheese-gatherers slowly lowered the empty bronze lamp to the ground. The crowd gasped—the lamp, thoroughly polished, gleamed like gold. Quangster and his companions stepped forward and began loading cheese into the basin. The crowd held its collective breath. Then Dounster stepped forward and spoke quietly to the cheese.

There was a blinding light, and *lak lak* mice and one human shielded their faces. When Hercules looked up again, many mice had tears in their eyes. "Thanks be to Ulrich," they shouted, and Hercules shouted with them. They had all experienced a miracle. Hercules looked over to Quangster to see his reaction. He seemed quite overcome, especially compared to the other cheese-bearers beside him, who stood idly by, licking their fingers.

Suddenly Hercules felt Olfer touching his shoulder. "Come, my grandson," he said. "While the others celebrate, the Stewards have work to do in the library." He took Hercules by the arm and motioned for him to lead, but Hercules hesitated, transfixed by the tumult all around him. A great revelry was suddenly under way. Fangster came bounding out of a house holding an immense bouquet of brightly colored balloons, and soon all of the young mice who were not absolutely blind and hairless (as mice say) were thronging around him, jumping for the strings. Out of nowhere, a twenty-piece band appeared and the town square was transformed into a dance floor. Soon all was in motion—the mice, the balloons, the instruments—all weaving and interweaving in a frenzy of celebration; and, above it all, the new sun burned with a bright white light while the newly polished brass of the lamp flashed with a golden fire.

Despite the exhilarating beat of the festive and patriotic songs, the enticing smells of cotton candy and fried seeds, and the energizing heat of a hundred dancing bodies, the old mouse seemed unmoved. "Come, my grandson," he said again, urging Hercules forward. "It is time." Hercules walked on, but his eyes were still fixed on the commotion. He accidentally trod upon the old mouse's paw. "Carefully, my grandson," Olfer reminded him gently.

Hercules apologized, but he couldn't hide his disappointment. "It all looks so . . . so—"

"Yes," said the old mouse, "it is your first relighting. *Lak* suns ago, I felt the same. But when you accepted the job of Little Steward, my grandson, you renounced the pleasures of other mice."

"I did?" whispered Hercules.

Olfer smiled grimly.

"Today you will find out just how many," he said. "Today is the day of truth for you, my grandson. Now that you have seen the relighting of the sun, you are old enough to know everything. After today, you will be different from all other mice."

When they entered the Steward's chambers, the old mouse laid the white-bound Chronicle on the table and sighed. "I have carried the Chronicle for the last time," he said. "At the next sun it will be your turn, my grandson. But for today, let there be light for you."

To Hercules' astonishment, Olfer began throwing open the room's iron shutters with surprising strength. The bright light of the new sun streamed in. The old mouse moved from window to window, and the clank of the opening shutters rang like a drumbeat in Hercules' ears. Finally the old mouse came to the last pair. Opening them, he revealed an iron box set in a niche in the wall. He brought it down to the table and placed it before Hercules. Slowly he opened it, his blind fingers fumbling at the clasps. A scroll lay at the bottom, wrapped in black cloth.

Perplexed, Hercules looked from Olfer's still face to the scroll on the table. "What is this, my grandfather?" he asked. The faint music of the celebration came through the open window like the pleasant sound of a distant storm on a lazy summer afternoon.

"My son," said Olfer, "*this* is the Chronicle of mice. It is now time for us to add a new entry. Unroll it to the end." Bewildered, Hercules complied.

"Now write, 'A human has come to live among us, for the first time.'" He waited until he heard the scratch of Hercules' finger on the paper, and then he sat down.

"Have you finished?" he asked.

"Yes," said Hercules, "but I don't understand. Why didn't we make this entry in the other Chronicle? Why do we make it here?"

"Turn back to the beginning and read, my son," said Olfer, quietly.

With a growing sense of dread, Hercules did as he was told. In a few moments, he looked up in horrified bewilderment. It was like the Chronicle, but not like the Chronicle. The words on the scroll were a sick mockery of reality. It began with the great heroes, Ulrich and Orcster, but this Chronicle spoke of bitter feuds as Orcster objected to Ulrich's growing power. It told of rumors of secret communications with an ally to raise Orcster's authority over all others; and then it told of the arrival of an enemy who made off with Orcster, bleeding in its jaws, and the destruction of the city down to its foundations.

"Yes, my son," the old mouse said to Hercules' open-mouthed silence, and his voice was sad but kind. "It is true. Those cities you saw, they were overrun and ravaged by rats."

"Rats!" cried Hercules.

"Yes, rats," the old mouse repeated. "Most mice who know of rats think they are just monsters invented to frighten children with. But today your eyes are opened, my son. There are rats, and there are cats, and no mouse is safe within the walls or without."

The hairs on the back of Hercules' neck began to prickle. A cold chill seized his innards.

"So you knew?" he asked. "You knew all along about the cities, about the rats? Why didn't you—"

"Read," the old mouse said again. "Read your history."

With a kind of sick fascination, Hercules read on. He read of famine, of destruction, of feuds between mouse and mouse. He read of the attacks from the rats, with no warning and no time to prepare. He read of the survivors searching for a new place in the walls to build a new city. He read of how they re-created the same terraces and built the same buildings and lived the same lives, as if nothing had happened and nothing would happen again.

He felt sick. He looked out the window at the bright new sun shining on the carefree city, where the mice—his friends, the mice—danced in cheerful oblivion.

"Why isn't this in the Chronicle?" he asked, finally.

"This *is* the Chronicle," the old mouse replied. "This is the Black Chronicle, the Chronicle of the Few. The Chronicle you read before is the White Chronicle. It contains all that *most* mice need to know."

"What do you mean?" Hercules burst out. "Don't all mice deserve to know the truth so they can prepare? There must be ways to prepare. . . ." The distant sounds of celebration came through the window. Now they sounded to Hercules like the ominous rumors of thunder. He shuddered.

"Listen and understand," the old mouse said. "*Lak lak* suns ago, the wisest mice met. They called themselves the Council of Three. They discussed and debated long into the night. Mice were not happy. They were ruled by their fear. Suspecting destruction at every moment, they lived lives of the hunted. They made nothing and saved nothing. Neighbor neglected neighbor, my son. Mice thought only of their own survival. The Council of Three considered deeply. They neither ate nor drank for three days. Then they finally agreed—only a few needed to know the truth of our existence.

"And so they helped the rest forget, my son. They confiscated all the scrolls about the attacks and put them under the control of a Librarian. They created a Censor to make sure not even the comics spoke of rats except in humorous situations.

Finally, they explained to parents their duty to protect their children from fear. Within two generations, all believed it horribly rude to speak of rats or cats or other inescapable dangers. And things improved. As life appeared sweet, mice made time for the sweeter things. They turned their minds to baseball and the comics. They splurged on mice cream. Neighbor took time to be kind to neighbor. Enjoyment flavored every detail of our lives."

"But it's not *true*," Hercules protested bitterly. "They're all living a lie! There *are* rats! There *are* cats!"

"Yes," said the old mouse, "but who knows if any of our children or our children's children will ever have to face them? The rats might as well live in another place or in another time. The Three were very wise, my son. Mice do not need to know."

"But what if the rats come again?"

"*When* the rats come again, we will do what we have always done," the old mouse said. "Most will die; some will escape. They will go to the Box. Yes, the Box. It does exist. It is exactly where you have been taught to find it."

"The Box?" Hercules repeated in confusion. "What's inside the Box?"

"It contains the kernel of our civilization," the old mouse explained, "the heart of who we are. Orcster's son made it after the First Destruction. It is hidden after each Destruction in a place that rats cannot reach. It has a lock that only mice can open. Inside are copies of the two Chronicles, the Black and the White, and the secret of how to make cheese burn. It contains all that mice will need to know to make a new city, as we have done time after time. The place where it is hidden contains some food and water and copies of books from the library.

Blindness stopped me from copying more. You should begin that work tomorrow, my son. The library must be preserved."

"But what if mice find the Box, but they can't read?"

"The Council of Three worried about that point, too," the old mouse replied, "and so they encouraged the comics. A few mice will always know how to read. Probably they will be among those who find the Box. They always have. . . ."

"I *knew* everyone should know how to read," Hercules said under his breath.

"You ask too much of other mice, my son," the old mouse said gently. "Someday, someday soon, you will be their Steward. They say the Steward is the Mother of the Mice. A mother does not tell her blind and hairless everything. She knows what to tell and what to conceal. This you must learn, my son. You must protect them from fear. Your every action should be like the lullaby that banishes the monsters of night."

"But who will do that for *me*?" asked Hercules.

"My son, your courage will sustain you. Your duty will be like a shield against fear. You have no choice. You will be the Mother of the Mice."

Hercules gave no answer—there was no answer he could give. But inside his head a little voice shouted, *How can I? How can I? How can I?*

"There is one last task for you to do on this Sun-Day," said Olfer quietly. "Go to the Box. Go and copy the new entries into the White Chronicle and the Black and then your Sun-Day will be over. Then go home and think. This will be a difficult night for you, I suspect."

There was a sadness in his voice that Hercules had never heard before. He looked over at Olfer's whitened eyes and saw that they were filled with tears; he knew the old mouse was weeping for Hercules' lost innocence. Reverently, he kissed Olfer's paw and stood. "Congratulations on seeing the sun lit for the *lak*th time," he said, trying to keep the tremor from his voice. "May you be in health until the lighting of the next."

"You will find the strength within you, my son," the old mouse said, as if answering the tremor and not the farewell. He stood up painfully from the table and slowly began to close the shutters. Hercules shut the door gently behind him. He had no idea where to find the Box, but he knew someone who would help him. He needed Quangster.

As Hercules walked back to the city, his indignation and astonishment over what he had heard began to fall away to expose the terror underneath. He had always known of the existence of rats, of course, but now the image of the fangs and claws and naked tails of the enemy suddenly appearing in his safe haven kept flashing before his eyes, and he half expected to see the rats around every corner. He tried to shake off his fear, but his heart pounded in his throat, and the skin crawled on his neck.

It did not help that the city was as silent as a ruin. The celebration had worn every mouse out and they slept where they had fallen. Dancing couples dozed, locked in their embraces; here and there parents curled around their blind and hairless babies; mice slept in uncomfortable attitudes around the tables in the cafés. The sounds of contented snores came from every open window. Standing over the sleeping mice, Hercules suddenly felt very protective of them all.

Quangster still lived with his mother (one of Gangster's great-granddaughters) in a house near the city square. When Hercules arrived, he found its door wide open as well as every window. It was considered bad luck to shut out the first light of the new sun. Everyone slept within, but Quangster was not among the sleepers. Hercules continued down the hall until he came to the open back door. There was Quangster, staring at the new sun with tears running down his cheeks. Hercules stood and watched him. The new sun burned with an exquisite brightness, like the purity of a white star shining on a winter's evening. But Hercules had no time for poetic notions; the burden of his mission weighed heavily upon him.

"Quangster," he said, "I need your help. Olfer the Steward has sent me to the Box. Do you know which box he meant?"

"Of course, Uncle. All mice know about the Box as soon as they are not absolutely blind and hairless."

"Then help me, Quangster. Take me to the Box."

"I cannot go there, Uncle!" Quangster said, the horror showing clearly on his face. "My time has not yet arrived. They say that we will know by signs and portents when our time has come."

"*Please*, Quangster!" Hercules cried. "I need you. *Olfer* needs you. He has sent me—"

But Quangster merely shook his head in agitation. "Some mice even say we are only to see the Box when we die," he explained nervously. "That is why we say that mice pass 'beyond the Box' when we mean to say that they are dead. I cannot go now—I must wait for the sign."

Hercules' sickening fear of the rats and his guilt at pressuring Quangster burst out of him all at once. "That's just a myth, Quangster!" he insisted. "Believe me! Being asked by the Steward is sign enough! Why would he ever try to hurt you? The Steward is the Mother of the Mice!" Quangster was panicking now. The brown of his eyes was drowning in the whites. Hercules felt terrible. The old mouse had said that his duty would act like a shield, but now he was using it as a sword against Quangster. Still he pressed on. "You *must* go, Quangster! It is your duty."

"If you demand that I go, Uncle," Quangster said, bowing his head, "I will of course follow you, out of love for you and for Olfer. I will admit that I am terrified. But after all, it is the greatest honor to give your life for the good of all mice."

Ignoring Hercules' protest that there was no danger, Quangster led the way through the upper levels of the city until they came to the mayor's residence at the edge of town. Behind it, a little passage led away from the buildings and turned a corner into the darkness. Quangster recited the directions under his breath as they followed the branching passage this way and that, upward and downward, past wires and pipes, and around joists and beams. The passage began to narrow until they had to crouch down. First Quangster and then Hercules dropped to all fours. The walls closed around them. They were indeed in a place where no rats could fit. Then Quangster stopped so suddenly that Hercules bumped into him.

"The Box is here," he said reverently.

"*Thank* you," Hercules sighed in relief. "I couldn't have found it without you, Quangster."

But Quangster wasn't listening; he was still overawed. "We have arrived at the Box, Uncle, and I am still alive." He was breathing heavily.

"I told you it was fine. . . ." Hercules began, but then he looked at the Box more closely. It was made of iron, and very heavy. Pictures decorated every surface. Some showed the sweet simplicity of mouse life: the fountains, the gardens, the celebration of a new Sun-Day; but these were interspersed with pictures of a different nature: of rats jumping from the highest level of the city down to the town square, the broken body of Orcster the Six-Toed Metal-Maker dangling from a rat's jaw. . . . Covering the pictures as well as he could, Hercules turned to Quangster.

"Can you open it?" he asked, still trying to shield Quangster from the pictures.

Quangster looked pained, but he slipped his tail inside the lock. In a moment, the Box creaked open.

Hercules knelt down and took out the two Chronicles. Taking his pencil from his pocket, he wrote down the new entries in his ugly script. Then he returned the scrolls to the Box and shut it with a clang.

"Can you tell me how you found this place?" he asked, taking out the map he had made on his first journeys.

Quangster, still awed, nodded and repeated the instructions he had learned as a child. Hercules wrote them on the map in English.

"My uncle," asked Quangster curiously, "what is that script that you are using?"

Hercules looked at him in surprise. "I ask because it doesn't look like the writing on the other side of your paper," Quangster explained.

Hercules had almost forgotten the nonsense words he had copied down from the towering wall. But strangely, the familiar symbols on the back of the map that had seemed like gibberish before suddenly formed words in front of his eyes. In a moment, he understood. He had always tried to read them from right to left, bottom up, as mice read, but this time his eyes had scanned them as if he were reading English, from the upper left to the lower right. He began to read the backwards tailscript out loud, but his voice trailed off after the sixth word.

"Uncle, what is it?" Quangster whispered.

"Nothing," Hercules answered quickly. But his heart froze as he finished reading the words in silence:

I, UKBAT, CLAIM THE THRONE OF RATS. I HAVE SLAUGHTERED THE MICE AND TAKEN THEIR SKULLS FOR MY SCEPTER. MAY MY REIGN BE AS LONG AND BLOODY AS MY FATHER'S. MAY MY SONS KNOW THE GLORY OF BATTLE AND THE SWEET TASTE OF MOUSE BLOOD UNTIL THAT GLORIOUS DAY WHEN WE HAVE DESTROYED EVERY MOUSE FROM WITHIN THE WALLS. LONG LIVE THE EMPIRE OF RATS AND UKBAT ITS KING!

For a long moment, Hercules looked at the words and at the hideous iron decorations on the Box. He thought of his mice sleeping so happily under the new cheese-sun, and he looked at Quangster, so faithful and trusting. . . . and at that moment he vowed that he, Hercules Amsterdam, would save them all.

FOR HERCULES, THE NEXT FEW WEEKS passed in a whirl-wind of worry. Since reading the message from the rats, he was determined to be prepared for the next attack. Even when he tried to convince himself that the rats might not come for years, he felt the inevitability of their coming like a noose around his neck. He felt in desperate need of an ally to fight against Olfer's pessimistic view that nothing could be done, and he saw no one but Quangster who might be of some help. He brought Quangster to the library and taught him how to read. But though it was often on the tip of his tongue to tell Quangster about the choking danger that daily tightened around them, he kept his silence.

"There will be time enough to tell Quangster if he becomes your Little Steward," Olfer reminded him.

"I won't need a Little Steward for a long time yet," Hercules answered automatically. The idea that he himself would be Steward someday filled him with dread.

"So why ruin his peace?" asked Olfer. "He does not yet need to know."

Finally Hercules dared to ask what had been on his mind for so many days. "Why *not* tell the mice and let them prepare? If we are to lie to them, why not give them a useful lie and tell them that we will survive if we are ready?"

"You are not the first of the Stewards to suggest it," the old mouse said, reasonably. "Kudzy Sentipeder, who was Steward before me, agreed with you. She went against tradition and tried to tell the younger generation. Most refused to believe her. Those who did believe grew frantic in their worry. They took extreme measures. Some fled and met uncertain fates—others did worse." He shook his head. "Besides, my son, there is no preparing. Even if the rats did come in our lifetime, what could we do but run?"

That's always the strategy of blind mice, Hercules thought bitterly, but he said nothing.

"Let Quangster stay happy," the old mouse urged.

And Quangster was happy. He was more than happy. He was blissful. Once he could read, it was as if he were addicted to reading. The two of them spent long days together in the library, reading side by side, as Hercules scoured the scrolls for hints of success against the rat attacks and Quangster greedily devoured first the comics and then the more serious treatises. Occasionally Hercules would lay down the depressing scroll he was studying and stare with envy at how Quangster's whiskers twitched with satisfaction as he read.

"How do you decide which scrolls to read?" Hercules asked one day.

Quangster gave a sheepish grin. "I'm trying to read them all, Uncle," he said, and then ducked his face to avoid Hercules' astonished stare.

He had made a good start. Since first learning to read, he had finished all the comics in the library's holdings and then all the medical treatises, from the diagnosis of brittle whiskers to the highly contagious *anstedan*, a disease of the tail. He was currently working his way through the obscure topic of geoponics: the practice—unknown within the walls—of growing food in dirt instead of water. Before the new sun's fire had cooled to its usual yellow, Quangster had worked his way halfway around the library's curved foyer. By the time Sangster's granddaughter's first granddaughter was born (occasioning a huge party that lasted for three days), he had finished them all. Hercules heard of his feat with amazement.

"He did *what?*" he asked Etchel.

"He's read them all," Etchel repeated. "Every scroll in the foyer. He even read my books—and unlike most mice, he seemed to appreciate their genius. Of course, he can't read any books behind this desk, not until he has permission from the Steward. They're restricted. Nevertheless, it's an impressive feat."

"Do you ever think of becoming Steward yourself, Quangster?" Hercules asked one day as they sat beside each other in the empty library.

Quangster looked down at the floor and gnawed on a claw. "Every day," he said. "It would be an honor beyond compare to serve my mice and to spend time here, with you and with the scrolls. I love the library, you know. I love holding the whole world here in my paws, in these books." He smiled happily. "Life is so good, and it's all thanks to you, Small Ears—" He stopped himself and added hurriedly, "My uncle."

Despite Quangster's attempts at formality, Hercules felt that something had changed between them. Soon Quangster forgot to add the words *my uncle* to everything he said; without noticing it, they had become equals. And before too long, they became something better than equals. They were thoroughly and undeniably friends.

Not long after, when a mouse born at the lighting of the new sun was suckling babies of her own, a sad event made them not only friends, but colleagues. The old mouse had been failing ever since he had closed the last shutter in the Steward's chambers. Hercules suspected that he had conserved every ounce of strength to see the sun relit and unburden himself of his lonely secret. When Hercules entered the Steward's chambers, he often found the old mouse asleep at the table, his wrinkled paws holding an ink bottle he would never need again. It made Hercules weep to see Olfer wither before his eyes. Sometimes he would take his teacher's leathery paw between his own two hands and give it a respectful and thankful kiss. Then the old mouse would open his blind eyes and sigh.

"It is not much longer before you will take up the Steward's mantle," he said one day. "Are you ready for the challenges? I have taught you all I could."

"I will never be ready," protested Hercules. "If that's what is keeping you going, you should know that I will always need you. Don't leave me, Grandfather!"

"This is foolish talk, my son," Olfer scolded gently. "If the rats came tomorrow, I could not see them. I would not be able to take more scrolls to the Box. You must be the one to lead the mice—it is your destiny and your duty." He grimaced then and put a paw to his chest.

"What is it, Grandfather? Can I help you?"

"There is no help for me anymore, my son. Leave me now. I must rest."

A few days later, Hercules passed Etchel coming down the stairs from the Steward's chambers. He gave Hercules a quick, guilty look and tried to push by him without speaking.

"I heard the Steward calling," he explained when Hercules took him by the arm.

"Was he looking for me?" asked Hercules, glancing anxiously to the door at the top of the stairs.

"He is now," Etchel said. He wrenched his arm out of Hercules' hands and ran down the steps back to his desk. Hercules raced up the stairs and threw the door open. In the darkness, he could barely make out the old mouse, huddled on a seat beneath the niche where the Black Chronicle was kept.

"Is that you, Oraclees?"

"Yes, Grandfather. Do you need something? Etchel heard you call out—"

"Etchel was here," Olfer said seriously. "I needed an answer to a question that has worried me these past few days, Oraclees. I have worried about the human. He has not left us, has he, my son?"

"No," said Hercules, "I don't believe he ever wants to leave. He wants to be a mouse, just like us."

"I worry about him, my son. He may want to be a mouse, but he is a human. He should not stay here. He should return to his own kind."

"Never!" Hercules exclaimed passionately. "I—he wants to stay here forever! He loves the mice—he. . . ."

"I feared as much," the old mouse said sadly. "Come here, my son. Let me take your . . . paw." Slowly, Hercules slid his naked hand into Olfer's furry paw. The old mouse stiffened slightly. "I did not think Etchel would deceive me," he said. "We leave deception to rats, cats, and humans. Try to lead my mice well, Oraclees. You are all they've got." And then he died. The light behind his eyes dimmed, and his limbs grew still, while the tears streamed down Hercules' face.

They postponed the usual ceremonies until Hercules was able to speak without a painful lump in his throat. He gave the eulogy at Olfer's funeral, but even as he spoke he knew his words were a small and awkward echo compared to Olfer's great confidence and eloquence. Then the mice who were interested (a mortifyingly small number, Hercules felt, largely made up of Sangster and her progeny) gathered on the baseball diamond and watched the mayor place the Steward's mantle over Hercules' shoulders. They clapped politely when Hercules announced that Quangster was now the Little Steward.

There were a few items of official business after the swearing-in. He presided over the marriage of a few dozen young couples and said a blessing over the blind and hairless in the audience, and then Ghin, the mayor, came forward to speak. Hercules sighed. The mantle felt heavy on his shoulders. He looked at Quangster's embarrassed but happy face and for a moment he wondered if he should keep his friend in ignorance. After all, as Olfer had always said, there was no reason to believe the rats would come in Quangster's lifetime. . . . But then he remembered the engravings on the Box and the message on the towering wall, and he knew it was time for Quangster to know the truth.

Once the few streamers had been removed from the grandstand and the handfuls of confetti swept up, Hercules took a deep breath and turned to Quangster. "We need to talk," he said. "Follow me."

He led Quangster out of the city and down one of the old passages. Quangster walked somberly by his side. "Last time we came this way, I ran away," he said. "I hope you have forgiven me, Small Ears. I was young. This time I will not run. Since I have seen the Box, something has changed in me. I feel. . . ." But his voice trailed off as the light from Hercules' lantern fell on the towering wall of letters.

"I cannot read it," he said simply.

"Read it backwards, from the top down."

Quangster squinted up at the tall letters and, with great effort, read them from left to right, top to bottom. Hercules could see that his whiskers trembled and his paws shook.

"I . . . I do not understand," Quangster said, after a long silence.

"I think you do," said Hercules.

"Are you telling me that this city was built by mice? Are you telling me that it was destroyed?"

"Yes—destroyed by rats."

"And the other cities you told me about, too?"

"The other cities, too."

"Is our city in danger?"

"I think so."

"Why is none of this in the Chronicle? Why have I never read about it in all those scrolls in the library?"

Hercules explained about the two Chronicles and the books behind the desk that were restricted to all but the initiated. "But now you are the Little Steward," Hercules concluded. "The books are now yours to read."

Quangster looked at Hercules' serious face and then back to the writing.

"I'd better get started, then," he said, and began walking home.

For several days, Quangster did not mention the rat warning but applied himself diligently to reading. He read as if nothing were different, taking out each scroll in turn and reading it carefully, absentmindedly sucking on the end of his tail. Hercules began to worry that Quangster was going to deny the threat—just as Sangster had refused to acknowledge the existence of the cat that had attacked her in the dollhouse. The loneliness of his responsibility settled upon him again.

Four days after they returned, Quangster asked to see Hercules in the Steward's chambers.

"I have been reading," he began.

"Yes, I've noticed," Hercules replied.

"I have come to several conclusions," Quangster continued. "The rats have come again and again to attack our cities."

"Yes," said Hercules.

"They attack without warning, and no one has ever been able to predict their coming."

"Yes," said Hercules.

"There seems to be no defense. When we are unprepared, we are slaughtered. When we are prepared, we are slaughtered."

"Yes," said Hercules.

"The Stewards have tried teaching the public and they have tried hoodwinking the public. In both cases, the cities were destroyed and only a small remnant survived."

"Yes," said Hercules.

"I have come to a conclusion."

"Yes?" said Hercules. To himself, he sighed. This was when Quangster would adopt the pessimistic resignation of Olfer and the Council of Three.

"We need help," said Quangster. "When Ulrich the Leader brought his mice into the walls, they struggled with darkness. The Chronicle tells us that Ulrich left the city and found a magic. We need to do the same. We need a magic to save us."

"That's brilliant!" Hercules exclaimed. "Why didn't I think of that? . . ." He was about to add, "since I'm so much older," when he suddenly realized that it didn't seem true anymore. He smiled again at Quangster and shook his head in admiration.

"The Chronicle doesn't say *where* he found it," Quangster went on seriously. "But I have faith that Ulrich will show us the way. We can find the magic, Small Ears. I am sure we can find it together."

Immediately, they began scouring the scrolls to find any mentions of Ulrich's magic. Quangster harassed Etchel again and again.

"As I've told you before," Etchel said, in his most tired voice, "the index says there was once such a book, but it has long since disappeared. No one knows how or when."

"Surely *you* can find it, Etchel!" Quangster wheedled, but Etchel could not be convinced to leave either his desk or his manuscript. Before long, Hercules despaired of ever finding the correct scroll. Given how many times the library had been destroyed, it seemed impossible that the particular scroll they needed would have been rescued every time. While Quangster searched, Hercules returned to learning what he could about rats: their habits (disgusting), their strengths (numerous), and their weaknesses (unknown). He read of the futile resistance put up by the mice, the puny weapons they had developed, and how none of it ever made any difference.

Things only got worse. One day, as he and Quangster worked together in the Steward's chambers, he had an awful realization. Quangster was busy going through a huge pile of scrolls, and Hercules was trying to memorize the Black Chronicle, as Stewards were required to do. He was summarizing the events of each sun on a separate piece of paper when a pattern suddenly formed. He checked it again. There was no doubt. The rat attacks came with a horrifying regularity—every seven suns, like deadly clockwork.

"Why hasn't anyone figured this out before?" he asked Quangster. "It's right here—every seven suns!" He pounded the table beside the scroll for emphasis, and Quangster jumped.

"What are you saying, Small Ears?" Quangster replied, confused. "I don't know that word you're using."

"Which word—" Hercules began, and then he remembered. "Do you mean to say that because mice can't count past three, you've been surprised by every rat attack?"

"It's possible, Small Ears," said Quangster, "but I don't understand what you are saying. Perhaps you could explain it to me."

Hercules found that his heart was pounding. He took a deep breath to settle his shaking hands. Then he ripped a piece of paper into ten pieces and laid them down. "One, two, three," he counted in mouse-squeak. Then he took the fourth piece. "Humans have a number for this one, too," he said. "We call it *four*." He took up the next. "*Five*."

Quangster was staring at him, shaking his head. "I almost understand," he said, "but I feel like there's a cloud before my eyes."

"It's okay," Hercules said. "I'll try something else." He laid out three pieces of paper, then three more below them, and then three more beneath *them*. "Look here," he said. "One, two, three, as you know. The rest are *lak*, right? But you can see that the *lak* are broken into groups of three." He paused to make sure Quangster was following. Quangster's brow was furrowed. His paw curled around his tail as it always did when he was thinking hard.

"Let's call this second row *lak*-one," Hercules went on. "We'll call this number one-one: the first *lak* number. This number is one-two, the second *lak* number. And this, one-three. Those are the first three numbers after three."†

Quangster looked, and squinted, and thought, and then, with super-rodent effort, pointed to the third row. "This is *lak*-two?" he guessed. "And we call the numbers two-one, two-two, and two-three?"

Hercules stood up and did a little dance. "Quangster," he marveled, "you must be the first mouse ever to count past *lak*!"

"No," Quangster answered, without looking up from the paper where he was writing the numbers. "They say that Ulrich could, too." He chewed on his claws as he contemplated the paper. "So after two-three, then three-one, three-two, and three-three! I see, Small Ears! But why are you showing me all this?"

†See the appendix.

"Well," said Hercules, quickly numbering the items on his list, "look at this. I'm just putting numbers next to each sun, and I'll start over every time the rats attack. One, two, three, one-one, one-two, one-three, two-one. Attack. One, two, three, one-one, one-two, one-three, two-one. Attack, again. One, two, three, one-one, one-two, one-three, two-one. Attack. It happens every time in the two-oneth year."

"So we can predict the attack!" Quangster squeaked. "This time, we can be ready! We can meet them with . . . with . . . whatever it is that we find to protect ourselves with. When will the next attack be, Small Ears?"

Hercules scrolled back through the Black Chronicle, looking for the most recent attack. "One, two, three," he started. "Four . . . five . . . six. . . ." He looked up at Quangster gravely, and Quangster's eager face fell. "It will happen soon," Hercules said. "It will happen in this sun."

There was nothing either of them could say. They could raise up an army and wait for their foes, but given the state of their present defenses, the only things they could muster up for arms would be some shiny brass instruments and the sheet music for a few festive and patriotic songs.

IF HERCULES HAD THOUGHT he'd been anxious before, it was nothing compared to the constricting fear that squeezed his heart now. He could not sleep at night, and he began to feel a constant cramping in the pit of his stomach. When he walked through the peaceful streets of the mouse city, he was overwhelmed with sadness. He loved the mice. He thought of Sangster's sweetness to him and how kindly Olfer had always treated him; he thought of Quangster, whose very skeleton was formed of integrity and friendship; he remembered the ecstatic celebration at the relighting of the sun; and then he saw it all destroyed by the claws and jaws of rats. Why end all this happiness, this peace, the little pleasures of creatures who would die all too soon, even without interference? He felt drowned in sadness that someone would want to lash out at something so fragile and so good (if the pleasures of friends and family, of festival days and days of doing nothing in amiable company could be called good, and Hercules knew in his heart that they were).

He went to visit Sangster. On his way he passed the café where they had spent so many pleasant hours together. Old mice—mice who had played baseball with him only last summer—sat hunched at the tables in the city plaza drinking mice tea and talking over old times. A few waved arthritically to Hercules as he hurried past. He saw Fangster among their number. Wasn't it just a few months ago that he had bounded out of a house carrying balloons with all the energy of a man in his prime? And now those few months sat on him like decades.

Sangster's house and yard were, as usual, crowded to the brim with her children and grandchildren and great-grandchildren and their innumerable offspring. They all seemed more somber than usual.

"What's wrong?" Hercules asked the nearest mouse, who was staring blankly into space.

"It's Grandmother," the mouse said. "She's passing beyond the Box."

"Sangster? Dying?" Hercules cried. "Has there been an accident?" Sick with horror, he pushed inside the house, squeezing past dozens of Sangster's children and grandchildren and great-grandchildren, until he reached the bedroom. Bangster was standing beside the bed, holding on to Sangster's paw. Hercules knew from his expression that he was too late to say good-bye.

"Oh, Sangster," he whispered.

Bangster leaned over and kissed Sangster's forehead. "She lived a long, fine life," he said in a low voice.

Hercules was suddenly enraged. "No, she didn't!" he contradicted. "She was practically blind and hairless when we first met, and that was just last summer—"

"Yes, all those generations ago," Bangster agreed, ignoring the anger in Hercules' voice. "She bore *lak lak* litters of mice. It was a good life." Then he turned his back to Hercules and bent once more over his wife; he whispered thoughts to her dead ears that were not for others to hear. Slowly, Hercules backed out of the room, and then he ran.

He hardly knew where he was going until he found himself at the baseball diamond, back where he had met Sangster for the first time, back where she had acted as catcher to his pitcher. Thinking of those days made his eyes burn with tears. He had loved her very much. She was the first creature who had not asked him to be something he was not. She had been his first friend. And yet their friendship had been so short. Too short! It was unfair—horribly, inexcusably unfair—that her life had run out. By his calculations, she was not much older than a year. Had she been a human, she might not yet have even learned to walk.

He wandered for a long time through the gardens and by the edge of the lake where she had gently goaded him onto the swinging vines. He thought of their days together, of the time they had spent poring over the pictures in the comics and the walks they had taken in the gardens. He thought of her grace as she had tripped across the narrow bridge at the top of the cavern with no fear of falling. He thought of the way she had smiled down so tenderly at her first litter of blind and hairless. He thought of her *lak lak* descendants. With an ache of sadness, he realized they would all be dead before he himself hit puberty. He suddenly felt a great desire to see Quangster.

"I heard," Quangster said, when Hercules found him in the Steward's chambers. "Poor Small Ears. I wish I could help. I know how much she meant to you."

Hercules sat at the table and said nothing. He looked at his friend miserably.

"She lived a full life," Quangster began, sitting down beside Hercules. The light from the cheese lamp fell on the fur of his head.

"Quangster! Hercules cried. "You have gray hairs in your fur!"

Quangster examined his fur unconcernedly. "That's hardly surprising—my littermates already have children and grandchildren and great-grandchildren. I suppose I am a *quastbuck*," he said, using the mouse-word for mice at the height of their lives.

Hercules opened his mouth to speak, but he found that he had nothing to say. Sangster's face swam before his eyes. "Your lives are too short," he declared bitterly.

"They are long compared to a mayfly's," Quangster replied. "And it is long enough for a mouse, I suppose." He rerolled the scroll he was reading before sliding a new one out of its ornate cover. "Come, we have work to do," he reminded Hercules gently. "This might be a good book for you—the index lists it as the most optimistic of the anti-rat treatises—" Suddenly he leaped up from the table. "Look! Look! Look!" he shouted. "Take it, Small Ears, I can't—" He fell back on his chair, one hand pressed to his chest, the other holding the scroll out to Hercules.

It was just a scroll, but inside the scroll was another, smaller parchment. Hercules reached out for it and began to read. "I, Ulrich, left the mouse city in the darkness to find light. . . ." His eyes flew up to Quangster's face in amazement. They had found the secret of Ulrich's magic.

The scroll was so old that the paper crumbled under hands and paws as they read, and the tail writing was strange, but together they eagerly deciphered every word.

"It was Kitty Joas who told him," Quangster said, in an awed voice. "I should have known—if the nightmare about the rats is true, then the promise of Kitty Joas must be true as well. . . ."

"Who is Kitty Joas?" Hercules asked. He was surprised to see that Quangster's eyes were full of tears.

"She is a Tugot, a fairy," said Quangster. "They say those who find her can ask for wishes. But no one has been able to find her for all these many years, the stories say. Oh, I always *hoped* those stories were true! Perhaps she will be able to help us!"

Hercules looked back at the scroll. "We *might* be able to follow Ulrich's directions," he said doubtfully, "but . . ."

"Let us go now, Small Ears," Quangster said eagerly. "A mouse lives for only a blink of an eye."

It was an old cliché among mice, but Hercules shuddered. "All right," he agreed. "I think I still have sleeping bags from when I used to camp out with Sangster. They're back at my house."

On their way out, they passed by Etchel, who was sitting at his desk, staring into space. His tail drooped, as if it had not been used for a while, and the dried ink on its tip was flaking off.

"Guess what, Etchel!" Quangster cried. "Hercules and I have found the book we thought was lost! We have found Ulrich's book, Etchel! It tells us where he found the magic! It was

Kitty Joas, Etchel! Kitty Joas herself, not from the ballads, but real!"

Under this onslaught of enthusiasm, Etchel's habitual look of disdain was replaced by a look of surprise, but slowly his supercilious mask settled back onto his face, and he took up his usual attitude of superiority and scorn.

"I'll enter it into the index, of course," he said, "but you know as I do that there are many books about those who have tried to find Kitty Joas and failed—even those with maps."

Loaded with sleeping bags, food, and water, Hercules and Quangster began their journey. It was the third time they had entered the empty passages between the walls together, but now it was Quangster who hurried ahead, urging Hercules to move faster. As they ran along, Quangster told Hercules all he had ever heard of Kitty Joas, of her magical powers and her invisible palaces, and his voice took on the singsong quality of a child recounting a favorite fairy tale. But their journey soon hit a snag. The passages twisted upward and downward, not at all like they were described in the scroll. Ulrich had said that they would walk until they came to a right-hand passage that went up steeply, but unless he meant a left-hand passage that went steeply down, it was not there. Hercules bent over the copied directions and frowned, but no matter how many times he made Quangster back up and start over again, they could never find the right path.

"I guess we might as well go back," said Hercules dejectedly as he slid to the floor in exhaustion. "There doesn't seem to be any point to this. For once, I think Etchel is right."

"Don't give up hope," Quangster urged. "We must be doing something wrong. Ulrich would not mislead us. Leaders do not mislead their mice."

Hercules snorted at that, thinking of the Council of Three, and wryly rubbed his aching feet.

"You know," Quangster said suddenly, "perhaps we should go back, after all. We forgot that today is Dounster's retirement. Little Daboonster is taking over his responsibilities, and it would seem odd if the Steward were not there. Don't worry—we'll try again afterward. We'll find Kitty Joas, Small Ears. We will."

"Sure we will," Hercules said, but he didn't believe a word of it.

They were among the last to arrive at the cheese-gatherers' hall. Inside it was very festive. The lamps had all been filled with soft-burning Gouda for the occasion, and Quangster seemed quite transported as he breathed in the smell. Hercules was unmoved. The disappointment of not finding Kitty Joas weighed heavily on him, and he was in no mood for sitting on a dais and hearing mice praise the wonders of cheese in song and verse.

The ceremony began with a blaze of cheese-burning, and then Dounster stepped back from the great basin in the middle of the hall and came to bow before Hercules.

"Steward," he said, "the stores of cheese grow low. Is this an auspicious time to go for more?"

Hercules stared at him blankly. He had no idea. He was not even sure if he knew what *auspicious* meant. Not for the first time, he wished that Olfer were still Steward. *I guess so* did not seem to be the appropriate response. He looked toward Quangster for help, but Quangster merely smiled back encouragingly, waiting for Hercules to speak.

"Yes," Hercules decided. Why should one time be better

than another to get cheese? "Yes, Dounster, it is an auspicious time. You should go at once."

Dounster bowed once more and called out in his tired voice, "Dinster! Dalinster! Eskabinster! The time has come for you to serve your mice. You know the way." Three young mice dashed out the door. Then the fanfare of trumpets announced the arrival of Daboonster.

As Hercules sat there, trying to keep his face stewardlike, his mind wandered. He thought of cheese and the cheese he had brought within the walls and how gently Sangster had lifted it out of his hands to take it inside and make a lamp of it. It occurred to him that it was a good thing that the first city he had come to within the walls was this living city. If he had stumbled first on the burned-out ruins, he might have given up. He never would have met Sangster or Quangster or any of them. And it was pretty amazing that he found the living city first, given how many ruins there were. . . . Then, in this vein of thought, he suddenly saw the nugget of a sparkling idea. He caught himself from calling out just in time. Dounster was standing now, praising Daboonster and her commitment to her mice. He looked old and tired and spoke so slowly that Hercules wanted to scream. He felt he would explode if he couldn't talk to Quangster soon. He tried signaling and making all sorts of subtle hand movements so as not to disturb the dignity of the proceedings, but Quangster merely signaled back that Hercules was disturbing the dignity of the proceedings and should cut it out.

As soon as they were off the stage, Quangster turned to Hercules and scolded him. "What were you thinking, Small Ears?" he said. "You nearly embarrassed yourself."

"We were wrong!" Hercules shouted back. "We were wrong, Quangster! Ulrich's directions weren't meant to start out from *this* city—but from *his* city. The map might still be good, Quangster! When we find Ulrich's city, we'll find her, I'm sure of it! We'll find Kitty Joas!"

So now it was all very straightforward. They would locate Ulrich's city amongst all the ruins in the walls; they would follow the landmarks they hoped had not changed over the intervening generations; they would find Kitty Joas' invisible palace; they would somehow convince her to help them—and that would be that. Optimistically, they shouldered their knapsacks, told Etchel that they would be gone some days, and set off.

The first challenge, of course, was how they would know Ulrich's city when they found it.

"It'll take us forever if we try the directions from every city," Hercules argued. "There's got to be some way we can figure out which city was Ulrich's just by looking at it."

"Maybe he left his name somewhere," Quangster suggested.

"Mice don't exactly go around signing their names on things," Hercules pointed out.

"Orcster the Six-Toed Metal-Maker did," Quangster said defensively. "It says so right in the Chronicle, 'Orcster the Six-Toed Metal-Maker made a lamp. He signed his name in gold.'"

Hercules reached over and grabbed Quangster's paw. "You were next to the lamp when it was filled—did you see his signature anywhere?"

"No," said Quangster. "We all remarked how smooth and unblemished the brass was. There wasn't a mark on it. It worried me, at first, but I figured it out. Though we *say* that we use the same lamp that Orcster made, of course that isn't true. His lamp is hanging empty in some desolated city. It must be very beautiful—they say no mouse between the walls ever reached his level of skill—"

"Don't you see?" Hercules interrupted. "If we find the lamp with Orcster's signature, we'll know we have the original city! That detail wasn't useless after all."

With renewed energy, they tramped on toward the closest city ruins. Although Quangster had seen them before, his whiskers drooped as they picked their way through the ash to the upper levels, where the view was best—and worst. "It's so much like home," Quangster sighed. "Even the paths that lead out of the city are the same—this one to the Box, that ladder there—but what's this?" Unlike the other passages, which ran beside pipes or bunches of wires, the path they stood beside came straight through a beam—as if bored by tools and rubbed smooth by careful hands. There was something about its smooth surface that made Hercules shudder, as if a rat were walking over his grave.

"I don't like it," he said, anxiously. "Let's check the lamp and get out of here."

The empty lamp hung crookedly from two of its chains. They creaked and moaned as Quangster worked the pulley to lower it to the ground. Hercules imagined the rats tipping out the cheese and greedily devouring it—he hoped they had burned their tongues. The light from their lanterns flashed and danced on the bright surface, but the brass, still shiny after all these years, was smooth and unmarked. There was no signature. It was not Orcster's lamp, and it was not Ulrich's city.

"It's never the first one you come to," Quangster said encouragingly. "Let's go on."

Apparently it was never the second one you came to, either, nor the third, nor the one-oneth. None of the lamps in the cities Hercules had discovered bore Orcster's mark, and there seemed nothing else to do but to search for other ruins within the walls.

It was late afternoon, as they were following an upward-leading trail toward the attic of Hercules' house, that the attack came. They had turned a corner when suddenly Hercules felt himself lifted high into empty space. Even though his ears were filled with Quangster's piercing shrieks and his sides ached where the clawed fingers dug into him, there was a strange peace in being lifted so high, like being cradled by his mother, so that even the flash of huge, yellowed teeth did not frighten him. Then something soft whipped by his arm, and he had the impression of a huge, fluffy tail. "It's okay, Quangster!" he called. "It's not the rats at all! It's squirrels!"

The squirrel who had picked up Hercules laid him down

again. "A thousand apologies," she said. "My eyes are not as good as they once were—I took you for one of my own blind and hairless. How embarrassing!" The other squirrels chattered soothingly to Hercules and pressed a walnut-shell goblet of crab-apple wine into his hands to steady his jangling nerves. When Hercules could breathe normally again, he looked around him with interest. It was apparently a family party. Festive nut-oil lamps were placed around the chamber, and great piles of uncracked acorns stood on the tables.

"We're so sorry to interrupt," Hercules began. "You see, we were looking for Kitty Joas. . . ."

"Kitty Joas, the Tugot?" one squirrel asked with interest. Though her accent was strange, the words she spoke were the same as mouse-squeak—it seemed to be the common tongue within the walls. "I've always heard that her palace is invisible. It has been many nut harvests indeed since any squirrel knelt before her."

"We are determined to find her," Quangster explained. "It is a matter of life and death. If she is as great as they say, she will not turn us from her gates."

"She will not have to turn you away," the squirrel pointed out, blotting her mouth with her tail, "if she can simply make sure that her gates cannot be seen."

"We will find her," said Hercules boldly. "But we must beg your pardon and hurry on."

Once away from the squirrels, Hercules turned to Quangster in excitement.

"I think I've figured it out," he said. "Of course we wouldn't find Ulrich's city up here, near the roof. Squirrels come from trees into the attic, but Ulrich didn't live in a tree—he lived on the ground. He would have entered the house on the ground floor. We need to go *down*, Quangster. That's where we'll find Ulrich's city."

"That's wonderful, Small Ears," Quangster exclaimed. "Of course you're right."

Following Hercules' new logic, they searched for passages that led ever downward. Twice they came to unfamiliar ruins, but in both cases the lamps did not bear Orcster's mark. Discouraged, they lay down to sleep, curling up in the corner of a passage small enough to keep rats from reaching them. Though neither mentioned it, they both twitched throughout the night at the unfamiliar sounds that can only be heard in darkness.

The next morning, they entered a section between the walls that made them both uneasy. They had found a network of copper pipes that seemed a reasonable landmark to follow, and it led by the open mouth of a large iron pipe that had been sawn off an inch or two above the floor. It led down into the darkness, giving off a terrible stench. Hercules and Quangster covered their noses as they peered into the dark depths. Even their whispers were magnified to booming shouts when they spoke beside it.

"I don't like it," Quangster said, grasping Hercules by the arm and pulling him on. But Hercules lingered. A strange compulsion came over him, and before Quangster could stop him, he had picked up a piece of broken plaster from the floor and dropped it into the pipe. It fell and fell for a long while in silence before they heard its distant *plop,* followed by what sounded like a squeak or a hiss from far below.

"Let's go quickly," Quangster insisted, and Hercules did not object. Neither felt comfortable until they were far away.

That afternoon, they found one more mouse city. "Lucky two-one," Quangster said as they made their way through the ruins. But it proved impossible to examine the lamp, for it was not there. The chains dangled from the cavern roof, but the lamp itself was gone. Hercules and Quangster examined the passageways to see if they could identify any of the landmarks from Ulrich's journal, but strangely, the tiny path they would have taken was gone, too. Instead, there was another one of the strange, smooth passages that ran right through the wooden beams instead of along them.

"I guess it can't be this city, either," Hercules said dejectedly.

"These smooth tunnels are so odd," Quangster reflected. "They don't—well, they don't *feel* like they were made by mice." Hercules agreed. There was something sinister about the perfect roundness and flawless smooth surface that made him feel uneasy.

Soon afterward, they came to a place that sounded as strange as the smooth tunnels had looked. It was never entirely quiet within the walls, of course, with the water rushing through the pipes or the creaking of the old beams as they settled. Occasionally they might hear the barking of the neighbor's Yorkies or a burst of canned laughter from a distant TV. But this was a new sound, a sound like children crinkling cellophane between their fingers. It seemed to come from a place behind a beam, and as Hercules went to investigate, his exploring hand broke right through the wall of the passage. A deafening shout of triumph filled the air, and a huge herd of carpenter ants came rushing through the hole.

Hercules shrank back. The ants came up only to his knees,

but their cold eyes seemed menacing and their serrated mandibles looked very sharp. They pressed around Hercules and Quangster, once or twice knocking them off their feet, but they seemed not to notice the travelers. Suddenly there was a piercing whistle, and Hercules and Quangster found themselves being borne away on a huge river of ants who were quickly flooding back down the smooth tunnel through which they had come.

The crush of ants carried them around a corner, and they were suddenly standing in an immense gallery. Tapers lined the walls, giving off a soft green light. In the center of the room stood a towering throne made entirely out of yellowed beeswax, studded with bits of seeds and wheat. The ant queen was sitting there, jet-black and magnificent, with delicately veined wings hanging down her back like a mantle, and a crown of butterfly scales upon her head. Quangster fell to his knee and bowed. Following his lead, Hercules made an awkward bob.

"Strangers," said the queen, using the common language in a raspy voice that was very hard to understand, "I am Hormigüe, Queen of the Ants. You are right to kneel in awe before me, for I am mighty. But where I am mighty, I am also merciful. Stand to your feet and answer. Why have you come?"

Hercules took a deep breath—he had never addressed royalty before. "Your most glorious majesty," he said, "may you live forever. We are strangers in this land on a mission. We search for Kitty Joas."

"The Tugot?" asked the queen. "We hear of her only in story and song. It was many thrones ago indeed that any knelt before the Tugot. Here, sit before me. I will sing to you of those days." Clapping her uppermost feet together, she shouted,

"Some accompaniment!" Three young ants ran into the great hall, dragging a huge cricket on a leash. Hercules shrank back. Though the cricket had a dull expression in its huge eyes, it was very large. When it began to rub its legs together, the noise was deafening. Over the din, Hercules could just barely hear the queen's ballad. The song went on so long that his head began to hurt and his cheeks ached from trying to keep a polite smile on his face.

When Hormigüe was done, the three attendants dragged the cricket out of the royal chamber. The queen seemed very pleased with herself. Turning back to Hercules and Quangster she purred, "Your kind is strange to me, and you must have traveled far. You must rest on your journey—let me show you the hospitality of ants." She called out to the servants that ringed the room: "Bring in a banquet for me and my guests! Find the best that the storerooms have to offer! Make sure you bring us plenty of honeydew. These travelers will be thirsty. Do not dawdle like drones, my daughters."

In a moment, the room was filled with ants carrying tables and chairs of exquisite delicacy and workmanship. Hercules had never seen such skillful woodworking in his life. Each piece was fashioned in the most beautiful proportions and decorated with tiny scrolls and carved sprigs of wheat. He and Quangster praised the furniture effusively, and the queen savored their compliments with a smile. More ants came in bearing carved wooden platters heaped with seeds, which made Quangster's mouth water, and then more with wooden jugs full of a clear liquid that proved to be sweeter and more delicious than anything Hercules had ever tasted.

"What is this, your highness?" he asked.

"It is honeydew, stranger," she responded. "Have you never drunk it before?"

"I've had a fruit by that name," said Hercules, "but it does not taste the same."

"I should think not," the queen answered indignantly. "This is no fruit drink, but nectar freshly squeezed from our aphids. It is the work of many of my ants to collect so much."

Both Hercules and Quangster put down their cups at that, but the queen did not notice. Four servants stood beside her, chewing her food for her and passing it directly into her mouth while she stared at the ceiling with a bored look on her face.

When the queen was full, she clapped her feet and called, "Clear it away!"

The servants whispered, "Yes, Mother-Highness," and quickly removed the plates and platters and tables. All of a sudden, there was a great clattering and clanking, and one ant servant was staring down at her four empty feet and the food spilled upon the ground. Two others quickly seized her and dragged her before Hormigüe.

"What happened, my daughter?" the queen asked, in a tone that seemed more tender and maternal than Hercules would have expected from her. "Was the platter heavy?"

"Yes, Mother-Highness," the little ant admitted, looking pleadingly up at the queen.

"Not *too* heavy, for you?" the queen asked again. Her voice was somehow less kindly.

"Not *too* much too heavy," the little ant amended hurriedly.

"No, of course not," Hormigüe agreed. "For a worker ant, a strong female worker ant, can carry six of her sisters, can she not?"

"Oh, yes, Mother-Highness—"

"Then perhaps you are *not* my daughter?" the queen asked solicitously. "Are you perhaps one of my lazy sons?" The young ant shook, and Hercules could see that she would be blushing red if only ants had red blood. "Ah, you claim you *are* a worker, not a lazy male drone?"

"Y-yes, Mother-Highness," the little ant moaned.

"And yet you act like a useless male. I will have no drones around me. You are not suited for work in my court."

The young ant's antennae quivered, and her mandibles trembled as she struggled to speak. "As you will, Mother-Highness. It has always been my pleasure to—"

"Silence!" shrieked Hormigüe. "You have disgraced your sex. Take her to the dairy!" The little ant's wails rang after her as she was pulled down the passageway.

Hormigüe brushed her four feet together as if she had just finished a distasteful task.

"I apologize for that lapse of hospitality," she said sweetly. "But now perhaps you would like to see the wonders of my palace?" Not knowing what else to do, Hercules agreed. The queen stood. Two young ants sprang forward to carry the wings that trailed behind her. Hercules and Quangster followed. As they walked, Hormigüe talked on and on in her rasping voice, pointing out the nurseries ("This is where I do my work laying eggs—a tedious duty, but it is the price of royalty") and the great royal storerooms, filled with seeds and bits of grain and great heaps of what Hercules suspected was Cap'n Crunch. They passed by the dairy, where hundreds of aphids, the ant-cows, were being milked. Quangster looked positively green beneath his fur.

"My chambers, of course, are the pride of the palace," Hormigüe was saying. "Come within, strangers, and marvel." They entered, and the room was indeed magnificent. The walls were lined with dark wood, intricately carved, and the whole room was suffused with a wonderful smell. Hercules could see in the center of the room an enormous golden basin that appeared to be filled to the brim with aphid honeydew.

"That is my bath, of course," the queen said airily, waving all four feet at it. "I believe it is quite famous, even in foreign parts."

Quangster walked over to the bath and ran his paws along its edge.

"Small Ears," he whispered in awe. "It is the missing lamp. Look! Here is where Orcster signed it." Hercules stepped forward and ran his hands over the elegant signature Orcster had wrought around the rim. Quangster closed his eyes to feel the perfect smoothness of the basin. "What a master! I don't think a mouse that followed him ever approached such perfection in his art."

The queen came up behind them. "You say *mice* made this?" she asked with interest. "The rats always claim that this is their work. Perhaps mice are not as stupid as the rats say. Of course, I have never seen a mouse—they may be quite different from their reputation."

It was shocking to hear her speak of the rats so easily, dropping the name of their enemies as if they were familiar neighbors. Hercules and Quangster stopped in their tracks, but Hormigüe went on, "The rats brought it once in lieu of a throne. I would not have accepted it, of course. *I* know the ancient contract. However, my predecessor was not so exact in her observation of her duties. Now come into this last gallery. Visitors travel from all over the walls to admire it."

Even Hercules and Quangster, who were still stunned by the sudden mention of the rats, could not remain unmoved by the gallery. The high walls were covered with pictures executed in inlaid wood. It was gorgeous. The detail was so fine, so exquisite that Hercules at first thought he was looking at sepia-toned photographs. Hormigüe narrated each picture in a bored voice, making it clear that the incredible murals were as familiar as wallpaper. "This is me at my coronation. Of course, I was shockingly young, the youngest queen since Hormiga-Ra. This picture is of Hormiga-Ra herself. It is quite ancient, from the founding of our dynasty. She was considered to be exceedingly beautiful. I look like her, do I not? These are the rats, of course, bringing the throne. It always amazes me that such clumsy creatures can produce a thing of such beauty. You can see from this picture how unmannerly they are. If it were not for the ancient contract. . . ." Her voice rasped on and on, but in their growing horror, neither Quangster nor Hercules was listening.

Even executed in wood, the rats were hideous. They were malignantly, horribly large. The final picture in the gallery showed a raucous banquet of ants and rats. Several rats were lying on the floor in a drunken stupor. Others were clinking wooden cups with ants in an apparent toast of mutual good wishes.

"This is after the rats destroyed a mouse city," Hormigüe continued. "Their celebrations are always excessive. They are the most uncouth creatures, but as I said, they are old allies."

"Do you think she knows that *I'm* a mouse?" Quangster whispered to Hercules in a low voice.

"I don't think so, but maybe I should do the talking," Hercules replied.

The queen was only too happy to bring them back to her great hall for another round of sugar cakes and honeydew (though both Hercules and Quangster asked to drink water), and there she questioned them closely about where they were from. Hercules prudently evaded the question.

"But tell me, your magnificent majesty," he said instead, using the biggest words he could think of, "what is the relationship between yourself and the rats you spoke of? Are they also under your imperial dominion?"

"Someday, perhaps," Hormigüe replied dreamily, "someday all the denizens between the walls may bow to me and call me Queen. But for now I am satisfied with my relations with the rats, though they are a noisy, ill-mannered lot. But what can you expect from creatures who let their males rule? Nevertheless, we have an arrangement. We have something they need, and they have something I like."

She rearranged her wings to show them to best advantage and began again. "I will tell you our history. Long ago, my people found a bees' nest between the walls. The honey contained within—" She cut herself off. "Of course, I was not even a grub in an egg at that time—it was thrones and thrones ago, in the time of Hormiga-Ra. But the histories say that the honey the ants found was as much more sumptuous than honeydew as a rat is bigger than an ant." A far-off expression came into her eyes as she spoke of the honey, and Hercules saw that dreamy looks had appeared on the faces of the servants around her. Finally, Hormigüe roused herself from her reverie.

"But the ants behaved rashly. They drove the bees from the

walls and devoured the honey. It was mostly the drones, of course. They are almost as stupid as fireflies. Even a grasshopper would have known to husband the bees to make the honey last forever. But honey drove the ants mad. When they brought more from the Outside, the ants left their work and stormed the storerooms. They killed the guards and gorged themselves, even to death. Those who lived pined for more. My foremothers realized that we must ban honey from our people."

Not knowing how to respond to this lengthy narrative, Hercules merely grunted and tried to look polite, but the false smile he had plastered to his face froze as Hormigüe went on.

"Then the rats came to us. They said they needed our services. They offered us a prize. Long ago, ant queens sat on thrones of wood, like common ants. But the rats agreed to bring us a throne of beeswax, scented with honey, to raise our majesty above that of all others. And so they have, ever since. When the throne gets old and brittle, and its honey smell is gone, they will return once more. It takes many reigns indeed for them to harvest enough wax, but they always return."

"And what do you give to the . . . rats in exchange?" asked Hercules, dreading the answer.

"We are ancient allies, the rats and ants," Hormigüe explained. "But the rats have an ancient enemy, the mice. . . . We find the mice for them and bore our tunnels right through the walls to their cities. You have no idea how clumsy the rats are. They *might* be able to find the mice on their own, but in so doing they would alert every mouse grub to their presence. Yes, the rats need us, and they are useful friends to have. They are gross and uncouth, it is true, but then again, they can work with honey without going mad."

"But how do you find . . . these mice?"

"We have hunters who track them by smell," the queen answered, "for mice must sometimes leave their city. As soon as the throne arrives, our trackers will spread throughout the walls. When they come across a mouse trail, they will follow it, and then the work of tunneling will begin."

Hercules was about to speak again when there was a sudden agonized cry, and one of the green lights at the end of the room flashed out. For a moment, the walls were filled with an angry buzzing like the beating of furious wings. Hormigüe clapped her feet again, and a servant came scuttling in. "Another firefly!" she commanded. Beside Hercules, Quangster moaned as he looked in horror at the green lights around the room. More servants were coming now, trying to subdue a struggling firefly at the end of a leash. One ant pulled the taper down from the wall and unceremoniously dumped a body out of the wooden cage at the taper's end. The team of ants forced the new firefly inside, and the cage was shut with a snap. The new firefly flashed a mournful flash, and then nothing.

"Impress upon him that he is to shine continuously," the queen said to the nearest servant.

"They can't last very long if they have to shine all the time," Hercules pointed out.

"No," Hormigüe agreed with a sigh. "They are an inferior species, but we have never found a better substitute. It is a constant struggle to keep them lit. We must punish them severely for their inadequacies."

Hercules turned to Quangster and saw his brown eyes were filled with tears. His desire to run away from Hormigüe (which had been rising ever since they saw the pictures of the rats) was now uncontrollable.

"We—we thank you for your hospitality," Hercules lied awkwardly, "but now we must go. We must find the Tugot. . . ."

"You will return, of course," Hormigüe said to them lazily, "and tell us where to find her. I will make it worth your while."

"We thank you for that," Hercules said, and he and Quangster sped out of the chamber.

When they could no longer hear the crinkling sound of the chewing ants, the two collapsed to the floor.

"I can't believe this!" Hercules exploded. "It just gets worse and worse!"

But Quangster seemed more upset about the aphids and the fireflies than about the precarious fate of his mice.

"I never would have believed that a living creature could be so cruel!" he cried out. "To treat those other insects in such a way. . . . To use them, rob them of their freedom. . . . Hercules, tell me the world is not so cruel outside the walls."

Hercules did not know how to answer. He resolved never to tell Quangster the origins of cheese.

They were both silent for a moment, and then Hercules groaned. "I think we have a bigger problem," he said. Do you realize that we have left a trail of our scent from the mouse city straight to the ants. . . . Once the rats come with the new throne, the hunter ants will not have to work hard to follow that trail."

Quangster looked pained. "You mean *I* left that trail," he said. "You mean *I* will be the destruction of my mice."

"No, I didn't mean that," Hercules said, laying a hand on Quangster's paw. "No, of course not. You will find Kitty Joas and save your mice. Don't worry, Quangster. Perhaps the rats will not come to replace the throne for many generations. It looked almost new, didn't it?"

But both of them could see the throne in their minds' eye, and, remembering how brown and how brittle it looked, they knew the rats would be coming soon.

IT WAS NOT UNTIL they were far away from the ants, covering and re-covering and re-re-covering their steps in a futile attempt to confuse the ant trackers, that Hercules realized that Hormigüe had solved one of their problems, at least.

"Would it cheer you up," he asked Quangster, "if I could tell you this minute the location of Ulrich's city?"

"It would, if you could," Quangster answered.

"Then follow me," Hercules said proudly. "We should return to the city with the missing lamp—that must be where Hormigüe's lamp came from. I understand now why we could not find Ulrich's original passage there, and why all the cities we've found have those strange, smooth tunnels leading from them. Don't you see? The *ants* made those smooth passages to bring the rats to our cities! But in Ulrich's city, the city with the missing lamp, their passage just happened to run into the one we wanted, and it hid the passage Ulrich took to Kitty Joas!"

Quangster nodded. "You may be right," he said. "I hope that you are right."

And Hercules *was* right. When they returned to the last city that they'd discovered before they came upon the ants, and followed the ant path for ten minutes or so, a rough mouse trail continued. Then the landmarks they had memorized from Ulrich's account suddenly materialized: a passage that went steeply upward, followed by a pipeway; and finally, Hercules and Quangster stood in the clearing where Ulrich had found Kitty Joas.

They stood for a long moment knee-deep in tattered newspapers, once used for insulation but long ago nibbled out for the private use of mice. They had absolutely no idea what to do next. The scroll had not said how they were to attract the Tugot's attention.

"Maybe she's dead," Hercules whispered. "It *was* a long time ago—"

"She's a Tugot!" Quangster replied in a shocked tone. "What could kill a Tugot?"

"Well, she seems to have misplaced her doorbell."

"Perhaps we're supposed to call out to her," Quangster suggested, and he began hailing her in his small clear voice, "Kitty Joas! Kitty Joas! Your children need you!"

Feeling a bit foolish at making so much noise, Hercules joined in. "Kitty Joas! Kitty Joas!" But the strange name felt funny on his tongue, and before too long he was calling, "Kitty Joss! Kitty Joes! Kitty Juice!"

Quangster gave him a disapproving look. "Perhaps I should do the calling," he said.

He stood in the middle of the clearing, his paws clasped behind his back, and began addressing the Tugot, using all the honorific titles he knew. He sang songs in her honor and made long impassioned speeches on the plight of her children. Then, his voice hoarse, he stood still and thought. Finally he raised his eyes to the ceiling and cried out, "Ulrich, father of all mice! Ulrich, tell me what to do!"

There was no answer; Quangster hung his head. Hercules sat down in defeat and put his head in his hands. Then suddenly, just as he was giving in to despair, he found—much to his surprise—that the dim light of their cheese lamps had exploded into the brightest sunshine he had ever seen. At the same time, the plastery walls disappeared, the scraps of newspaper vanished, and the confines of the passageway fell away. Instead they were standing in an extraordinary courtyard of shining alabaster columns, tinkling fountains, and graceful statuary. An immense artificial lake stretched out before them; a path of stones led across its brilliant surface to a little island.

They stared at each other. Hercules was speechless and Quangster's eyes were filled with wonder. "It's just as they said," Quangster whispered. "This is the palace of Kitty Joas."

"How did we get in?" Hercules whispered back.

"I don't know," Quangster answered. "I was thinking about Ulrich, and how he could count past *lak*, and how I have learned to count past *lak*—and I just counted."

Nervously, and nearly hand in paw, they approached the shores of the glassy lake. They could see that there was a small structure on the island, a bit like a gazebo in an English garden. Something dark was stirring within. Without thinking, they walked across the stepping-stones toward it—later Hercules commented that they could not have walked away had they tried. When they were no more than ten paces from the island, a black figure appeared and opened up its arms.

"Well come, my children," it spoke sweetly.

Quangster wobbled. He grabbed on to Hercules as if his knees had suddenly turned to water. "It is Kitty Joas," he murmured, half to himself. "She is even more beautiful than they sing in the songs."

"Yes, Quangster, it is I," said Kitty Joas. "And yes, Quangster, I am more beautiful than words can say. Some have even said that it is inaccurate to call me beautiful, but better to say that I am beauty itself. Some, too, have said that it is inadequate to call me powerful, but better to say that I am power itself. For me, I think there is no better description than to say that I am Tugot."

She stood up languidly, elegantly, majestically, and they could see that she sat on no throne, but merely on a pile of cushions and her own coiled tail. She was much smaller than Hercules had expected—not much larger, in fact, than a young female mouse. She was not exactly like a mouse, however, for her fur was a thick and silky black, like Hormigüe's coloring— except about the neck, where Kitty Joas' fur shone with a magnificent blue-and-purple iridescence. Two delicate antennae bobbed gently as she walked toward them, and her tail swept out behind her, long and magnificent, with all the feathery elegance of an ostrich-plume fan. The tiny paws she extended to them ended in nimble fingers covered with soft fur like black velvet, and her large jet eyes were serene.

"Well come, my child Quangster," she said again. "Well come, Hercules Amsterdam, from without the walls. You have reached your goal. I have opened my gates for you, although you needn't have come so far. As you will realize, my palace fills every crevice and corner of this world within the walls. Your own library, for example, lies neatly within the confines of my topiary garden. But I am glad you made the effort to come all this way. It shows the earnestness of your intent, and earnestness is something I value in my children."

"I don't understand," Hercules interrupted. "How can our library be in your garden? I've walked all around that area and I've never bumped into an invisible tree."

Kitty Joas fixed him with a cold look. "Invisibility is for common fairies," she said. "I am Tugot. My palace is all throughout the walls, as I have said, but it is not invisible. It is just as you see it—it is here, and your little cities are here, too. We are both here, in the same space."

Hercules opened his mouth, but Kitty Joas cut him off. "I know you don't understand, little human," she said. "But even you can understand that two people can stand in the same place, if they do not stand there at the same time."

Hercules' head began to hurt.

"We do not live in the same time, you see," she explained. "I am living in what you call the distant future. We can stand together only when I choose to let you into my time."

Hercules stood staring. Beside him, Quangster stirred. He knelt down on one knee before Kitty Joas.

"You know so much, my lady," he said with a quaver in his voice. "You must know why we have come."

"I do, little Quangster," she said, smoothing her tail over her shoulder. "You wish protection from my other children, the rats. But you do not know how you wish to stop them, nor do you know what you intend to give up in return."

"Give up?" broke in Hercules. "What do you mean, give up?"

"In payment, young Hercules. I always ask my children to give up something for my favors. It is only fair. If it is to be a big favor, I ask for something important, perhaps the most important thing of all."

Quangster nodded. "I understand, my lady," he said.

"I don't," said Hercules under his breath.

"I didn't expect you to, little human," Kitty Joas replied. "For you are not from within the walls. You do not belong here—you will never see what we see. It is right that my children sacrifice something. It demonstrates their earnestness and their gratitude. Ulrich, for example, sacrificed his friendship with Orcster. When the first rat king grew tired of being small and powerless, he gave up the beautiful hair on his tail—oh, it was lovely! I believe the royalty still makes all rats shave now, to make them all as ugly as the ruling family, as ugly as mice— begging your pardon," she said to Quangster. "Or perhaps you would like hair on your tail?"

Quangster shook his head. "You know I would not waste my wish on vanity," he said. "I am here to ask you to save my mice."

"And how would you like me to save them, little Quangster?" Kitty Joas asked in her sweet voice, looking deep into his eyes. "I demand that my children ask me for favors, not miracles. Tell me what you want me to do, and I may comply."

"I haven't figured that out, my lady," Quangster answered with heartfelt dignity. Then, so quietly that Hercules wasn't sure he heard, he added, "But I do know what I would give in return."

"Then perhaps *you* would like to beg a favor," Kitty Joas said to Hercules. "What is it that you want me to do for you?"

"Well, I . . . uh . . ." Hercules stammered, trying not to look into Kitty Joas' eyes. There was no sparkle in them—they looked as hard as marbles. "I just thought we'd make our plea, and you'd . . . do . . . something. . . ." He trailed off lamely.

"So you don't know how you would like me to help you?"

"I guess not," Hercules said, turning a little red. The coldness of her eyes bored into his. He felt as if he were getting an ice-cream headache.

"What about juminy juminy?" she asked.

"What's juminy juminy?" Hercules asked.

"Juminy juminy is a very old magic," Kitty Joas replied, settling herself on her cushions again. "It will make you big; it will make you small. That might help you, I suppose?"

"I suppose," echoed Hercules.

"Then I will give it to you," Kitty Joas said. She closed the fingers of one outstretched paw. When she opened it again, a pile of brightly colored pills rested on her palm. "Because you taught Quangster to count to seven, I will give you seven pieces. Use them well. A piece taken when you are small will make you big, *almost* as big as other boys your age. A piece taken when you are big will make you small, as small as you are now."

For a moment, Hercules didn't know how to respond. The bottom of his stomach seemed to have fallen out when she mentioned getting big; he honestly wasn't sure if he was excited or terrified. He pictured his parents' ecstatic faces when he appeared full-sized at the dining-room table, but then he immediately imagined how difficult it would be to convince them to let him shrink back to his proper size. He thought of the mice and the comfort he had first found among them, and he remembered his vow to protect them.

He looked at the bright juminy juminy in his palm, count-ing. "You can keep the seventh," he said, drawing a deep breath. "I won't ever take it. I wasn't meant to be big—I'm go-ing to live my whole life with mice."

"As you wish," Kitty Joas said disinterestedly, but she left all seven pills in his hand as she turned to Quangster.

"Now do you know what you want, my child?"

"I'm not quite sure, my lady," Quangster answered slowly. "May I have a little more time, time to go home and prepare and consider? Will you open your gates for me once more?"

Kitty Joas looked at Quangster with an expression that could almost have passed for pity. "You will return when you are ready," she said. "For me, it has already happened. Your future is in my past. If that is too complicated, my child, know this: I will honor my promise to you. When you need me, call, and I will answer. But now, my child Quangster, I know you and I know your desires. Shall I show my lands to you?"

"Beyond anything, I wish I could see their wonders," Quangster began, "but we feel the press of time upon us, and we must get back. We must find a way to protect our city from the rats."

"There is no need to worry—time does not pass in your world when you are here," Kitty Joas answered. "You are living in my time now. The rats will be no closer to your city when you return." She turned and led the way, with Quangster following in respectful awe and Hercules, still suspicious, trailing behind.

But Hercules could not be long immune to the astounding sights of Kitty Joas' land. It was magnificent. Or, as Kitty Joas might have said, it was magnificence itself. They soon came to her orchards, where trees no more than one foot high bore tiny fruits, just the size for mice. There she offered them fruits of every variety: apples, bananas, and oranges; grapefruit, lemons, and limes; peaches, plums, and nectarines; apricots, figs, and dates; mangoes, papayas, and cherimoyas; jackfruit and star fruit, all growing together under the magical sun. And the most amazing of all was that some trees were in blossom while others bore fruit, and others had just the beginnings of new leaves. And (as Hercules watched) the old leaves simply turned golden and disappeared without withering and falling. Before they had seen even a corner of her gardens, they left and crossed her meadows (covered with every imaginable wildflower, pollinated by tiny golden bees) and started over a mountain pass. Hiking high above the plains, Hercules occasionally caught sight of her geysers spitting foam high into the sky. When they grew tired (Hercules long before Quangster), Kitty Joas waved her little paws, and a cloth spread itself out on the fragrant grass. It was covered in an instant with dozens of delectable dishes: steaming corn, strawberries with powdered sugar, crispy french fries, vegetable soup, and chocolate cake. Hercules ate until he could feel his stomach swelling under his hand.

"We are almost at my eastern palace," Kitty Joas said, getting to her feet and waving the picnic away. Through a little copse of radiant birch trees, they caught sight of a towering building nestled at the base of a snowcapped mountain. A waterfall fed directly into its moat. As they drew closer, they could see that the building was a castle made entirely of brilliant stained glass. The castle seemed to be guarded by two huge green lions, which made Hercules a little nervous. But as they got even nearer (Hercules carefully hiding behind Kitty Joas and her swishing tail), he could see they were bushes growing in the shapes of lions. Behind them, he could see other bushes growing into spirals and arches and the shapes of mice, squir-rels, ants, rats, and pigeons.

"What is this place?" asked Quangster. "It is wonderful."

"This is my topiary garden," Kitty Joas replied. "Humans use shears and scissors to cut their hedges into shapes, but I have neither the time nor patience. My bushes grow in the shapes I require. They are pretty, are they not? I often come here. As do you—we are standing in your library now, and it is time for you to go home."

And they were home. Amazed, Hercules and Quangster stared at each other: they were standing beside the table in the Steward's chambers. The topiary garden was gone; Kitty Joas had vanished. If it hadn't been for the seven pieces of juminy juminy in his pocket, Hercules might not have believed that their journey had taken place at all.

"THERE IS MUCH TO DO, Small Ears," Quangster said, as quickly as if the words were already in his mouth when Kitty Joas had waved her paws to send them back.

"What? We're not even going to talk about what just happened?"

"After we are safe for good, then we can indulge ourselves in reflection," Quangster said, brushing his paws against each other like someone getting ready for hard work. "You have seen what I have seen, Small Ears. If we are lucky, we may have a generation left before the rats arrive, but that is only a blink of an eye."

Unhappily, Hercules agreed. He put his head down on the table. "I was so sure she was going to save us!" he moaned. "What are we going to do now—except watch our city burn?"

"We must redouble our efforts to find new defenses,"

Quangster began. "You, Small Ears, must consider how you can use your gift from Kitty Joas. And both of us should think of what favor I should request."

"Agreed," said Hercules weakly. The pocket that held the juminy juminy suddenly seemed very heavy. He shook his head as if to steady his resolve.

"And we need patrols," Quangster went on. "We need patrols to wander through the walls, confusing our scents to make the ant-trackers' job harder."

"Agreed."

"And we need other patrols to listen for the ants and crews to board up the tunnel as soon as it appears."

"Agreed."

"And we may want to create more safe havens like the Box, where mice can hide if we are unable to stop the rats. I intend to help every mouse escape. We may not save our city, but we will save our mice."

"Agreed."

"This all adds up to one clear first step," Quangster concluded.

"It does?" asked Hercules.

"We need a school. You were right, of course. More mice need to learn to read, to learn about the Black Chronicle, and to read the scrolls in the library. Even if our city is destroyed, they must be able to build a new one and start anew the work of defense. The time for secrecy is past. I know the Stewards have often been skeptical about the abilities of mice, but I know one mouse, at least, who would join our school. I have rarely met a mouse with such understanding. . . . She will be the first, but others must follow. Can you teach them to read, as you taught me?"

"I think so," Hercules answered.

"Then I will go now and find you students." And in a moment, before Hercules could respond, he heard Quangster clatter down the stairs, shrug off Etchel's surprised questions, and dash out the front door. It slammed behind him like an exclamation point.

Tiredly, Hercules pulled a fresh piece of parchment before him and reached into his pocket for his pencil. His fingers brushed the juminy juminy, and again his stomach lurched; he pulled his fingers out quickly and shook them as if they'd been burned. Then, without much enthusiasm, he began to make the kind of alphabet book popular among humans:

is for Gouda

is for Bat

is for Mice Cream

is for Cat. . . .

A smile crept over his face as he began to illustrate each of the twenty letters with drawings. Dreamily, he planned out future editions and imagined how much nicer the book would look if he could get his old set of watercolors into the mouse city. He closed his eyes to rest for a moment, thinking of the pleasure he used to find in painting with a little dandelion-fluff brush, and then his head hit the table. He was still sleeping many hours later when Etchel began banging on his door.

"The people are asking for you, Steward," he said. He was trying to look aloof as usual, but his paws shook and he seemed very pale.

Hercules followed him down the stairs. "What is it?" he

yawned. Etchel didn't reply. As they reached the foyer, Hercules could hear the sound of many voices talking all at once outside, sounding like the roar of the ocean. When he pushed the door open, a sea of mice rushed in. Their urgent paws pulled him outside.

There, on the ground, a little mouse lay on a makeshift stretcher. Hercules knew him slightly—it was Dinster, one of the cheese-gatherers. He was soaked with blood and shivering in a way that made Hercules very nervous. He bent down beside the stretcher. "What happened?" Hercules whispered, dreading the answer.

"We couldn't get any cheese," Dinster whispered. "It was the c-c-cat. . . . There really was a cat. . . ."

Hercules was suddenly filled with rage. "Get this mouse a doctor!" he shouted.

The mice stared at him blankly. "A doctor! A doctor!" he repeated. "You know, someone who can heal him!"

The mice all shrugged and whispered to one another. "We brought him here so *you* could heal him," one of them said.

"I'm the Steward, not a doctor," Hercules said wildly. "You can't expect me to know everything!"

"The Steward is the Mother of the Mice," another answered.

Hercules heard himself let out a yell of anger and then, not knowing what else to do, told them to bring the stretcher into the library. "Get Quangster," he said to Etchel and let the door slam behind him.

Hercules and Dinster were alone—there was no one to help him. The pigeonholes that lined the walls seemed like a thousand eyes watching to see what Hercules would do.

"Are you all right, Dinster?" he asked inadequately.

Dinster was shivering violently now. He seemed unable to speak. Hercules took off his jacket and laid it over the mouse. He patted him anxiously and looked around for help. One of those thousand pigeonholes must hold a book that would tell him what to do, but which? Frantically, he began pulling out scrolls at random, trying to find something helpful, and letting each drop to the floor when it proved useless. He found books on agriculture and comics about heroic mice; he found books full of love songs and books about Kitty Joas; he found books on the strategy of baseball and books on the treating of ingrown claws; he found books on the doomed friendship of Ulrich and Orcster, but nothing about how to treat a young mouse who had been savaged by a cat. More and more scrolls lay on the floor, surrounding Dinster as he lay shivering on the ground, and Hercules felt overwhelmed with helplessness and misery. Finally, he sat on the ground and cried. When Quangster returned, he found Hercules holding Dinster's dead paw and staring into space.

"I couldn't save him," Hercules said blankly.

Quangster reached down and shut Dinster's eyes. "Don't blame yourself, Small Ears. No mouse could have saved him."

"But I knew there was a cat," Hercules said, his voice cracking. "I sent Dinster right into its jaws. You were there when I sent them off . . . *you* saw. It didn't even cross my mind when Dounster asked. How could I forget the cat? If I really were the Mother of the Mice, I would never have let them go."

"They knew the risk," Quangster comforted him. "All the cheese-gatherers knew about the cat—it was the secret of our guild that we might meet a cat once we slipped under the door to find the cheese. Dinster knew what he was getting into. He did it for his mice. I would've done it—we all would have."

"*I* should've been the one to do it," said Hercules miserably. He jammed his hands into his pocket morosely and then yanked them out again as his fingers touched the juminy juminy. A sudden idea swept through his brain. "That's right. I *should* have been the one to get the cheese. I should be the one to get it now." Without saying good-bye, he raced out of the library.

He ran until he came to the hall of the cheese-gatherers. A group of mice was huddled there, talking in hushed tones about the accident and how to hide it from the rest of the mice. Hercules looked for some he knew. "Panster!" he called. "Punster! I need you!"

Two mice detached themselves from the group and came up to him. "Yes, my uncle?" they asked.

"I'm going to get the cheese," Hercules announced grimly. "I need your help." The two mice bowed and followed Hercules without another word. As they walked down the corridor in silence, Hercules practiced the apologies he would make for his role in Dinster's death, but nothing came out. When they reached the opening of the mouse hole behind the bookcase, all he could say to them was, "Wait here."

He stepped into his old bedroom and reached into his pocket. The seven pieces of juminy juminy were still there, oblong and bright, like little pills. Before he could change his mind, he popped a green one into his mouth. It was very bitter. He swallowed it hurriedly.

Immediately he felt the extraordinary sensation of being blown up like a balloon. In a moment, he was more than four feet tall. He stood there in disbelief, wobbling on his new, large feet and flexing his new, large fingers. He looked down at his small dollhouse and the miniature ladder he had made so many months ago. Then, full of angry purpose, he strode across the room and grasped the doorknob. The door that had always given him so much trouble opened easily in his hand. The cat was crouched outside, waiting, whiskers twitching. Hercules kicked at her with his foot. "Stay away from my mice," he spit at her through gritted teeth. Then he stormed past her toward the kitchen. His angry footsteps echoed throughout the empty house, and he realized with disappointment and relief that no one was home. It was just as well—he didn't have time for explanations. With a tug, he yanked open the refrigerator door.

Someone had just been shopping—the shelves were full of food. Quickly he scooped up bars and packages and little dried-up heels of cheese and hurried back to his room. He laid them just next to the bookshelf where Panster and Punster were waiting and sat back on his heels, triumphantly, his anger seeping away. This, at least, was something concrete he could do for the mice.

He expected them to be stunned, and they were. In one trip he had brought them enough to refill the sun and light every house for a generation as well. Panster and Punster squealed and clapped their paws, but to Hercules' surprise he could not understand what they were saying. Their words sounded like shrill squeaks.

"I can't understand you!" he called down to them, but he found that he could not make the proper squeaks with his new, large throat. Frustrated, he pulled out another piece of juminy juminy and was just about to take it when the room brightened. It was the sun coming out from behind a cloud. Hercules turned toward the window, shielding his eyes.

It was a spectacular spring day outside. The sky was a rich blue behind the fruit trees just coming into flower. Hercules walked toward the window as if in a trance; the fierce sense of duty that had propelled him out of the mouse city ebbed away. He had forgotten how wonderful it was outside—the brightly colored houses, the sounds of the birds, the smells of spring, and the laughter of children. The three boys he had watched so often were riding up and down the street on their bikes. They didn't look so frightening now that he was big. They looked happy. They were whooping and barking like dogs and looking as if they never worried for a moment that rats would burst into their city with bloody bared teeth and fearsome claws. Hercules stared, fascinated. He stood so long at the window that Panster and Punster must have thought he had turned to stone. They squeaked at him again.

"In a moment," he said absently, but they continued with their piercing little cries. "All right, all right," he said in mouse-squeak, but again, the sounds came out all wrong. He glanced toward them struggling to get the cheese behind the bookcase and into the hole, but he could not pull himself from the window. He wanted to see the boys on their bikes again. Suddenly he didn't want to just see them. He wanted to go out and *be* one of them; he wanted to be a full-sized human, if only for a moment.

"I'll just go for a minute, I promise," he said, in English, and then he walked out of the room and shut the door.

OUTSIDE! HE WAS OUTSIDE! It was even more extraordinary than Kitty Joas' lands. The colors were so bright they glowed—the yellow and red of the tulips; the orange and blue of the scowling pansies; the green, the glowing green, of grass and new leaves on the trees; and above it all the impossibly brilliant blue of the sky. And then there were the smells—lilac, cut grass, bread baking in the downstairs neighbor's kitchen. And the sounds—the whistled songs of the birds, the chirrups of the squirrels as they ran in and out of a hole in the attic, the pigeons cooing in the eaves, and, loudest of all, the intriguing shouts of the boys on their bikes as they raced up and down the street and around the corner.

Tentatively, Hercules took first one step and then another down the front stairs. In a feat of daring, he jumped down the last three steps all at once. He tingled with omnipotence; power and strength coursed through his large limbs. In one step—all in one tremendous stride—he stepped boldly over the massive roots of the oak tree in front of his house that he used to scramble over with so much scraping and difficulty. He lifted his giant leg again and took another step of immense proportions: he was standing before the flower beds. He reached down among the bees with one enormous hand and seized a tulip—a flower that he previously could have used as a beach umbrella. Now he plucked the velvet petals from the stem one by one and crushed them in his hands. He savored the sensation of rolling them between his fingers before he scattered them to the winds—and then he stopped. He looked guiltily down at the yellow pollen staining his hands and at the ugly bits of crushed petal, already turning brown. Why had he destroyed it? No reason—no reason, that is, beyond the fact that he could.

The boys were coming back on their bikes. They flashed by as if he were still only three inches tall, and when Hercules saw the expression on their faces, he was relieved they hadn't noticed him. He shrank behind a tree and watched with horrified fascination as the pack of them circled in front of a girl who was sitting on her front steps, reading a book. They were barking and yelling, "Dog! Dog!" at her, but she didn't look up. She read on calmly, and once she yawned, as if sitting in the hot sun had made her sleepy. A man came out of the house then, and the boys raced off. Hercules watched how tenderly the man tousled the girl's hair before getting into his car and driving away. The girl waved once and went back to reading. Hesitantly, Hercules walked toward her house and stood before her on the sidewalk.

She was not pretty. At best she was what was once described as plain. Everything seemed slightly wrong with her—her eyes were too close to her nose and her nose was a pudgy little knob above her crooked mouth. Her mousy hair was very thin and haphazardly held up by half a dozen small barrettes, but several locks of hair had pulled free and hung down limply around her face. She read very quickly, judging by how often she turned the page. Inside the house behind her, a dog was barking desperately.

"Hey—" said Hercules shyly.

The girl looked up and blinked behind her glasses. Her eyes were magnified to huge pale circles behind the thick lenses. "Hello," she said. Her voice was low and gravelly, and he recognized it at once. It was the girl who had been their guide in the school yard.

"What were they doing?" Hercules asked.

The girl jerked her thumb in the direction the boys had gone. "Those morons, you mean? Wasting their time if they think they're bothering me, I swear. Why do they think calling me a dog is an insult? I'll take dogs over most humans, any day."

"I'm a little scared of dogs," Hercules admitted.

"Really?" the girl asked. "I love dogs and dogs love me. I'm a veritable pied piper of dogs. I tell you, if I'm ever in trouble, all the dogs in my general vicinity will just flock to my aid. No kidding."

Hercules looked nervously over his shoulder, half expecting a whole pack of dogs to descend upon them.

"The one you hear barking inside there like a lunatic is named Princess, which I know is a dumb name, but I didn't give it to her. She's a bona fido German shepherd and a thing of canine beauty, let me tell *you*. She doesn't always bark like that—she just knew those boys were trying to bug me. Would you like to meet her? I'll have to know your name first, of course, if I'm to introduce you. *I'm* Juna Loch." She stuck out a hand and Hercules shook it shyly. It was soft and warm, very different from the hard paws of mice. He held on to it a little too long, and the girl gently pulled herself free with a little laugh.

"And you—?" she prompted.

"Hercules Amsterdam," he said. "What kind of name is Juna Loch? I've never heard it before."

"That's because I made it up," she answered. "I've been Juna Loch for eight months now. Before that I was Sally Albacore, but I ditched that name pretty fast, let me tell you. It says Ermengarde Ashland on my birth certificate, if you can believe it, which personally I cannot."

"Where did you get Juna Loch, then?"

"Out of thin air, where else, I ask you. I had to. No one could call me Ermengarde, not even when I was but a homely babe. How could they? Who in their right mind could look at a baby and call it Ermengarde? I swear."

"But what did your parents call you?"

"My mother didn't call me anything. Skipped. Flew the coop. Sad but true. My *fa*ther called me Dormouse." She rolled her eyes. "The indignity of childhood, I swear. Do you want to meet Princess now?"

Hercules felt a little weak in the knees. Swallowing hard, he lied, "I'd love to."

Juna Loch got up from her seat. Putting the book in the mailbox for safekeeping, she went to open the door. It was as if a tornado had been released from the kitchen. There was a streak of blackish brown, a fusillade of sharp barks, and Hercules found himself on the ground pinned down by Princess' hard paws. He saw his life flash before his eyes and it was unsatisfactorily short. Then Juna was hauling Princess off him, clucking her tongue, and admonishing the dog: "Down, Princess, I swear. My goodness, what will Hercules think of us?"

Shaken, Hercules got to his feet. "Show some manners, you big galoot," Juna upbraided her pet, forcing Princess to a sitting position by planting herself bodily on the dog's haunches. "Now shake hands and meet my new friend. You say howdedo, Princess." Princess gave a short bark and lifted one paw. "Come on, shake it!" Juna encouraged Hercules. Squeezing his eyes shut, he shook the paw, noting the claws.

"You don't really like dogs, do you?" asked Juna Loch, squinting at him.

"I've never really met one before," Hercules evaded.

"Really?" exclaimed Juna Loch. "Is such a thing possible? Have you been living in Outer Mongolia? On second thought, I would have thought they had dogs in Outer Mongolia. Mars, then. Have you been living on Mars?"

"Well . . ." Hercules began. "Not exactly. . . ." Juna was waiting interestedly, her head cocked to one side. "You see, I . . ." She smiled encouragingly while Hercules cast about for the right words. "Where I've been living . . ." he tried, and then he let it all blurt out. "You see, the truth is that up until this moment . . . I've been only three inches tall."

"*Really,*" Juna Loch responded. "How interesting!"

Princess suddenly started growling, baring her enormous teeth at a squirrel scampering in the yard. Then Juna grabbed the dog's collar before she could lunge after it. "Excuse me for a moment," she said, standing up and hauling Princess back into the kitchen by the collar. "Let me remove this large item so we can have some uninterrupted conversation." She delivered a resounding kiss to the top of Princess' head, then slammed the door shut. Princess took up her frantic barking again.

Juna Loch walked back to Hercules and plunked herself down on the front step beside him. She arranged her chin on her two hands and turned her full attention to him. "Three inches tall, you were saying? Tell me all about it."

So Hercules told his story, and as he spoke, Juna Loch's eyes grew even huger and rounder behind her thick glasses. "Oh, my!" she said, clicking her tongue and, occasionally, "Oh, *man!*" When he came to the part about Hormigüe, she interrupted to say, "I do not care for that individual," and when he told her about Kitty Joas, she raised her eyebrows so high that they disappeared under her mousy hair. "I can't say I approve of *her* behavior," she said. "If she really thinks of the mice as her children, shouldn't she try to take care of them a bit? What a way to run a railroad."

When Hercules had finished, Juna stood and stretched her short arms. "All righty," she said. "Want some lemonade?" Feeling deflated, Hercules stood alone on the front steps, watching her walk ungracefully back to the house. How could she think about lemonade? The relief he had felt there, in the sunshine, telling his story to a sympathetic ear, was swept away by guilt. He was ashamed to be sitting in the bright sunshine while Quangster was working to organize the school, while Panster and Punster struggled to haul the tremendous load of cheese to the storehouses, while Dinster was being laid to rest. . . . When Juna Loch came out, staggering under an overloaded tray, Hercules was already on his feet.

"I really have to go—" he began.

"In a moment," she said, rockily balancing the tray of sloshing lemonade on one hand as she sat down. "No point rushing off half-cocked. If anyone ever needed a plan, bud, it's you, I swear." She set down the tray and dug a notebook out of her pocket and clicked open a pen. "As I see it, your friend Quangster seems to have the right idea—except that his plan doesn't protect the city. Seems a waste to me. Well, I'll tell you, my dad always says that the best defense is a good offense. Or maybe it's the best offense is a good defense, I can't remember. But it all amounts to the same thing—we have to figure out the rats' weaknesses."

"And if they don't have any weaknesses?"

"Oh, come on, Hercules! There are no monsters without weaknesses! There's always the garlic, the silver bullet, or the stake through the heart. We just need to know what it is for rats."

"There's rat poison, I guess," said Hercules.

"But look here," Juna Loch broke in. "If we go in and try to kill them, that's just sinking to their level. We need something more elegant, more poetical. I don't know *what* yet—I've only just started to think about it. But I'm guessing that the rats know. A trip to ratville might be in order. Do you know where the rats live?"

"The comics say they live in the sewer pipe," Hercules answered, trying to keep his stomach from lurching out of his mouth. "But what do you mean, a trip to ratville?"

"I mean, we go find them. You and me. We'll do some reconnaissance. Espionage. Surveillance. You know. In the tradition of the great spies and detectives. That juminy juminy you've got, it can't make us invisible, can it?"

"No," said Hercules, a little bewildered by the whirlwind pace of Juna Loch's conversation, "but maybe you could ask Kitty Joas for invisibility."

"Nope, not me," Juna Loch said, shaking her head emphatically. "I've got no truck with fairies. They're bad business, I find. They always twist your words. Start with a fairy, and you end up with a sausage on the nose, I swear. I would like to see this Kitty Joas, though. I have an idea."

"We could go there right now," Hercules suggested, "if you don't have anything else to do."

"What else would I have to do that's better than this? Even if I had a plan for tea at Buckingham Palace, I'd cancel it to be three inches tall and see a Turbot."

"Tugot," Hercules corrected.

"Yeah, that. I can take some of your juminy juminy, can't I? Because I will certainly make it worth your while. This sort of thing is right up my alley, let me tell you." She stood up, shoveled two cookies into her mouth, and went inside. "Let me just make sure Princess has food and water. I wouldn't want her to starve just because I was being captured and tortured by rats."

She returned in a moment, buckling a wide belt around her waist. Every inch of the belt was covered with pockets or flaps or hanging pouches that slapped against her as she walked. Hercules could make out a flashlight, a coil of rope, a knife, a leather-bound notebook, and a flask, but there were other bulges and lumps he could not identify.

"I like to be prepared," she explained as Hercules stared at the belt.

"Oh," he answered.

"Well, let's go coordinate our efforts with this Quangster.

I'm all for coordinated efforts, measure twice, cut once, and all that. So lead on, Hercules Amsterdam. I'm right behind you."

Hercules began walking toward his own house. Juna trotted along behind him and soon edged her way to the front, talking all the time. "I brought a flashlight," she said. "And rope—you really shouldn't go anywhere without rope. What else. Asthma inhaler. Paper. Duck tape. Pepper."

"Pepper?" Hercules asked. "What do you think we'll run into? A hard-boiled egg?"

"Trust me," Juna said huffily. "I'll bet you thank me for this belt before our adventure's through. So this is your house—nice color. Where's the mouse hole?"

"It's upstairs—in my bedroom. We're the apartment on the second floor."

He opened the front door for her, thankful that it hadn't locked behind him. Juna Loch was up the stairway in a flash and through the open apartment door—he must have forgotten to close it in the newness of being big. The cat had apparently taken advantage of his negligence to sneak downstairs and was now huddled in the hallway. Hercules gave her another dirty look before following Juna into his apartment. She was already in his room, crouched down, looking behind the bookshelf.

"The mice seem to have managed the cheese already. I was going to offer to help. Is that your dollhouse? Will you fork over them juminy juminy now?"

Hercules handed her one of the little pills, and Juna swallowed it. She chuckled with amusement as first her arms and then her legs began to shorten. Her head deflated like a balloon and shrank down to the size of a pea, and then, with a faint *pop*, the rest of her body followed. "Yee-ha!" he heard her call from far below—she was doing a little dance. Quickly, he swallowed his own piece. When they were both the same size again, Juna said, "I never thought I would be doing *this* when I got up this morning, let me tell you. Oh, man! What a day!" It was at that moment that the cat came in and made a lunge for them, and they scampered behind the bookcase and into the hole. Juna Loch was holding her sides from laughing so much.

"I tell you," she said, "I haven't had this much fun since I don't know when. I'm awfully glad you came by, Hercules Amsterdam. Now lead the way."

And so with Hercules in the lead (though not much of one), the two entered the world within the walls.

12

WHEN THEY ARRIVED in the mouse city, they were met with great applause. Panster and Punster had returned with stories of Hercules' wonderful feat in cheese gathering, and mice who had only nodded to him before came up and hailed him as the Mother of the Mice. He was not surprised that they ignored Juna Loch, since mice consider it rude to notice the unusual. But he was amazed that Juna did not shrink from the mice. The first time a mouse her size approached, Juna shouldered Hercules aside and reached out to grab its paw. The mouse gave her an odd look, then hurriedly thanked Hercules before scurrying away.

"The mice don't make you nervous?" Hercules asked.

"Why should they?" she replied. "These are the good guys, aren't they?"

"It's just that most people don't really like rodents. . . ."

"Well," said Juna Loch, with a significant look, "I guess *I've* learned over the years that looks really aren't everything. But what are they *saying*? I can't understand a single thing. It's all squeak to me, I swear."

"It is?" Hercules asked, surprised. "Maybe your ears just need to get used to being small. When I was big this morning, I couldn't understand the mice, either. I guess I'll just have to translate for you—maybe your ears will adjust."

They walked through the city, searching for Quangster. Juna Loch took it all in with openmouthed amazement. Once down at the town square, she looked up at the cheese-sun hanging from the top of the cavern and at the mice scurrying across the wire bridges above them. She admired the terraced streets with all the houses painted pink and green, and her breath came through her teeth in a long whistle.

"Nice city, Hercules," she said. "So, what do they have to eat around here? I could stand to get the taste of that juminy ju-miny out of my mouth, I swear."

She was in luck. All around them, preparations for a public feast of thanksgiving were under way. Great platters of seeds were being roasted in the big public ovens by the baseball dia-mond, and the smell of celebration perfumed the air. They found a vendor selling little paper cones of mixed seeds, and Hercules bought some for Juna.

"They're tasty," she acknowledged, "but they seem to fill up the nooks and crannies of the stomach and leave a great gaping hole in the middle, don't you find? Where's this mice cream you're always talking about?"

When she tasted it, Hercules could tell she was disap-pointed. "What's this?" she asked suspiciously.

"Mice cream, like I told you."

"I don't mean to be impolite," Juna Loch said, "but this is certainly not cream and it is not exactly cold."

"I didn't say it was cold," Hercules said defensively, looking down at the sweet nut butter in his cup. It had always been the most delicious thing to eat in the mouse city, the thing he looked forward to after a long day, but now it sat in the cone, looking bland and unappetizing.

"Well, it's no *ice* cream," June said, definitively. "No offense, big guy," she went on. "I'm just saying there are some advantages to being human, and ice cream is definitely one of them. Well, break time over. Let's go."

They finally found Quangster in the cheese-gatherers' hall, overseeing the filling of lamps. "Don't use too much," Quangster was cautioning the workers. "Let us not use up in celebration the very thing we are celebrating." This was too complicated for the young mice. They nodded wisely at Quangster and proceeded to ignore him, piling the lamps full.

Quangster leaned over to the mouse beside him and said, "This is what I was saying, Marla. This is why I am sometimes discouraged." He—who had always been so shy—was leaning close to this strange mouse, almost putting his arm around her.

"Quangster!" Hercules called, more loudly than he'd expected. "I'm back! I've brought help from Outside the Walls. Come meet Juna Loch."

"Small Ears!" Quangster said. "I'm so glad you're back—I worried . . ." But Juna Loch had advanced and began pumping his paw up and down. Quangster's voice trailed off as he stared at Hercules for direction.

"That's the way we shake hands Outside the Walls," Hercules explained.

"I see," Quangster said, gamely trying to return Juna's salute. Then he took the paw of the small brown mouse beside him and pulled her close. "This is Marla Brisket, Small Ears. She is our first student. I have already told her everything. There are mice who will understand—Marla proves it."

Marla held Hercules' hand in her paw for a long moment, after the manner of mice. "It is an honor, my uncle," she said. "Quangster has explained what you have already done for us. We have not had such a leader since Ulrich himself."

Hercules blushed. Juna poked his side. "What are they *saying*?" she asked.

"She's glad you're here," Hercules said, still embarrassed by Marla's compliments.

"Well, tell them we can sign up for each other's fan clubs later," Juna said. "We have work to do and then some, I swear. This is war and we need a council of war. Where can we go to talk?"

They walked together through the preparations for the feast up to Hercules' house. Compared to the happy tumult around them, they were a somber group. Soberly, they gathered around Hercules' table. Hercules glanced at Marla Brisket. She was small and very pretty, and something about her coloring and the curious intelligence in her eyes reminded him of Sangster. She met his stare with a soft smile. "May I use this ink and paper?" she asked. "If this is a council of war, we should preserve it for the ages. It will be of great interest to future generations if we succeed, and of great usefulness to others if we fail." Hercules nodded, and Marla dipped her tail into the ink. She sat poised to write.

It was the time for great and moving words. Hercules

looked around the room for inspiration. It was just as he had left it. Several anti-rat treatises were strewn across the bed from the last time he had been home, only two or three days before. It seemed like weeks. The last time he had sat in his little house he had not even known about Kitty Joas; he had believed the responsibility of saving the mice lay squarely on his small shoulders. Now, after all his adventures, he was left with the same conclusion. He sighed, and raised his eyes. Three eager faces looked back at him, and suddenly he was encouraged. He threw back his shoulders and began.

"We *will* save the mice," he said boldly. "Look at what we have accomplished—we have doubled our numbers. We have Kitty Joas' promise to grant us another audience. Moreover, we have knowledge on our side—and determination." He paused, and repeated his words to Juna in English.

"I'm with you," she said, "but tell them my rules. I do not want to behave like a rat. If we're going to defeat them, I say do it elegantly and without violence or not at all. I would rather run than do to the rats what they've done to the mice."

Marla waited for Hercules to stop translating before she spoke. "I agree with this human," she said. "I will not seek them out to do them harm. I will not destroy my principles to save my life. We must prevent the rats from reaching our city or we must prepare to leave the city before they come."

"Marla has had a wonderful idea, Small Ears," Quangster began. "The mice in the cheese-gatherers' guild are already partly initiated. They already know about cats and humans. It is only natural that they be the first to learn about the rats. Moreover, thanks to the tremendous stores of cheese you secured for us, they have little to do. They are the perfect mice to become the first patrols."

Juna nodded encouragingly as Hercules translated. "Well, what do you think, Hercules? It seems less bleak than when you first explained it all to me. What part should we take for ourselves?"

The others stared at her. "Juna," Hercules said happily, "your ears must have adjusted. You were just speaking mouse-squeak. It was perfect, too, except that it sounded in the beginning like you were talking about herring."

"I'm squeaking in mouse?" Juna squawked. She smiled proudly, and then launched into more mouse-squeak; it was mostly intelligible. "But anyhoo," she summarized, "let's go back to the task at hand. What say you, Hercules? Shall we take over offense?"

"It makes the most sense," Quangster agreed. "You're the only ones who can walk in the walls without leaving any mouse trails to follow."

"Good point," said Juna. "Well, we'll take offense, then. No, we don't take offense at *you*. I meant, we'll take over offense as our job. I think we'll start with diplomacy, though I've never been a diplomat before. But how hard can it be? It's just talking. And talk, *that* I can do."

"What is diplomacy?" Marla asked.

"My father says diplomacy is the art of letting other people have your own way," Juna said. "It's when we try to talk it over, rather than fight. It's a very delicate business, let me tell you. I hope the ants will at least listen."

"The ants?"

"Yes, the ants. The rats cannot find the mice without the ants. But the ants have nothing against us—they only help the rats because the rats help Hormigüe. But if *we* help Hormigüe, perhaps she will help *us*. Of course, it's possible that we can work on the rats directly. We'll know more once we're in the sewer pipe."

"Once you do *what*?" asked Quangster and Marla together.

"We're going into the sewer pipe," Juna said, triumphantly. "That's where the rats live, right? Well, we're going right into the mouth of the lion to count its teeth. It's the best way."

Marla shook her head in admiration. "I say it again, Steward. You are a marvel."

"I'm not so sure about this plan to go to the rats," Quangster said, looking very worried. "Small Ears, do you think it's wise . . . ?"

Hercules did not think it was wise, but he felt Marla's confidence in him and swelled a little with pride. "We will have rope," he explained lamely to Quangster.

"Oh, yes-siree," Juna Loch said airily. "We'll have rope and we're prepared for every contingency, every eventuality, every possibility—except those I haven't thought of. But I assure you, I am very thorough. You have no need to worry, I swear. But we should get to it."

"And so the Council of *Lak* is adjourned," Marla said, finishing her writing with a flourish. "And may we all have the courage of Ulrich."

"And the luck of the lucky," Juna added.

"Good luck, Small Ears," Quangster said, coming to stand beside Hercules. He held his friend's hand for a long moment before turning to Juna Loch. "Please take care of him," he said to her in a soft voice. "He means more to me than I can say."

"Don't worry," said Juna. "I've never lost a boy in a sewer pipe yet."

Hercules watched the door shut behind the mice's tails and

sighed. Juna was busy checking the little compartments of her belt. "You don't have any human food here, do you?" she asked, looking around the room. "We might as well have another little snack before we go. All this talk of saving civilization makes me hungry, I swear."

13

JUNA HAD IT ALL PLANNED OUT. Their first stop would be to see Hormigüe. "Best-case scenario," she said, stepping on Hercules' feet in her effort to walk beside him in the narrow passageway, "Hormigüe listens to us and calls off the hunters: no tunnel, no rat attack. Likelihood low—but nice to imagine it could happen, though it might be too short an adventure, I don't know. We may have to take that trip to ratville after all."

"How—" Hercules tried to interrupt, but Juna went on in her businesslike way.

"Tell me more about this queen. What's she like?"

"Full of herself, mostly," Hercules said.

"The royal *we* and all that?"

"The royal wha—?" he asked.

"No," Juna corrected, "the royal *we*. You know, when kings and queens talk about themselves like they're more than one person. 'We are not amused,' 'we have to use the toilet,' that sort of thing. All part of the way they try to pretend they're different from regular people."

"I didn't really notice it, but she sure thinks she's special."

"Well, maybe you should take the lead here. I wouldn't be so good at talking to royalty. They get my dander up. I'm just too American, I guess. All created equal with those inalienable rights and all that. So I think you should do all the talking."

"All right," Hercules agreed, "but what do I say?"

"You are offering her what she has not," Juna said. "It's simple. Offer that the mice will supply her with cheese for light so she can get rid of the fireflies. In return, she doesn't build the tunnel."

"Juna Loch," Hercules exclaimed, "that's the most elegant solution I've ever heard. Quangster will be ecstatic."

"Thanks," she said briskly. "Hey, Hercules—I've just gotta say I'm awfully glad to be here. Have I said that yet? This is just about the best thing that's happened to me in years, let me tell you."

"I'm glad you're here, too," Hercules said, and he really was. Back in the darkness, creeping through the dusty passageways, the seriousness of their plight was somewhat eased by the friendly sound of Juna's talk. It was like the bells hikers wear to warn bears away, he thought. All the nameless fears that used to set his hairs to prickling seemed to scurry away from the jangling of Juna Loch's voice.

For much of the walk, they had long discussions about where to meet if separated and what kind of signs they could leave for each other on the walls if necessary. "There's just one other thing," she said. "Do you know pig Latin?"

"Pig Latin?" Hercules repeated. "No, I've never even been to school."

"I swear, Hercules!" she said. "You don't need to go to school to learn pig Latin. Listen. Isthay isway owhay ouyay eakspay igpay atinlay. Get it?"

"No," said Hercules.

"You mean O*nay*," June said. "That's how you say it, don't forget. Listen again. Isthay isway owhay ouyay eakspay igpay atinlay."

Hercules tried again. In a moment, he was fluent.

"Imay atherfay andway Iway alwaysway eakspay igpay atinlay," June said, "but it does get kind of tedious, doesn't it? Anyway, you'll meet my father when we're done with all this. He'll love you in an instant, and I hope you'll like him. He . . ." Her voice trailed off; they had come to Ulrich's city. Juna walked around it, her mouth open, but no sound came out. She looked depressed.

"So this is it," she said. "This is what they do."

"Every time," Hercules said. "It's the same in all seven cities we've found."

Her voice grew teary. "How could they?" she asked. "Why wipe out all this hard work, this nobility . . . ?"

She walked around slowly, looking solemnly up at the hanging chains.

"This is the city Ulrich founded," Hercules said. "This was where mouse civilization began."

"The poor mice," she said sadly. "Tell me about this place, please. It just reeks of history. Can you tell it to me as we walk?

Because we really should be walking. 'Miles to go before we sleep' and all that."

So Hercules told her how Ulrich had found life outside too harsh, too cruel, too short, and how he had found a hole that led to a paradise, where no winter crushed mice with cold, where no owls swooped, and where no cats ever pounced. He told her how Ulrich, along with his sworn companion, Orcster the Six-Toed Metal-Maker, had convinced others to follow. He told her of the founding of the city in the dark, and the need for light. He told her of Kitty Joas' magic and the subsequent struggles for power with Orcster, who had never acknowledged Ulrich's leadership and now objected to his being treated like a god. He told her of Orcster's treachery and the council where Ulrich had accused Orcster of endangering the city, only to be interrupted by the sudden and savage attack of the rats.

"What was Orcster's treachery?" Juna asked.

"I don't know," Hercules said. "The Chronicles can be very vague. If there were any books about it in the library, they've long been lost. But Kitty Joas said that Ulrich sacrificed Orcster's friendship to get the cheese magic."

"She did?" Juna asked indignantly. "This Kitty Joas! She's terrible! Why would she do that? Even fairies shouldn't behave that way—" A look of disgust had come over her face. "*What* is that smell?"

"We must be close to Hormigüe," Hercules said. They had come to the pipe where he had dropped the little bit of plaster. "We found this pipe just before we found the ants. I hate it— it's so, so. . . ."

"It's certainly less wholesome than oatmeal," Juna Loch said, peering into it and holding her nose. "I do not mean to insult your housekeeping, but something is rotten in this particular state of Denmark. Perhaps you should inform your parents that a little routine maintenance may be in order in the pipe department. That is one benefit of having diminutive progeny, after all. You can roam throughout the walls and tell your parents where upkeep is needed. For example, this particular pipe smells like it might go straight to the sewer—"

"Say that again?" Hercules interrupted.

"What, all of it? From where? I'm not sure I can re-create the free abandon of the original production, but—" Suddenly she turned around. "Forget the *smell*," she said. "What's that *sound*?"

It was the faint crinkly sound of the chewing ants. Hercules put his finger to his lips and peeked around the corner. They had come to a gallery where the ants were hard at work.

"Man, oh *man*," Juna whispered, and then the ants were upon them. As she had with the mice, Juna kept her composure, but Hercules was alarmed by their reception. At their first meeting, none of the ants had taken any notice of them, but now the two humans were escorted directly, and not gently, to the great hall.

The room was still lit by the angry green light of the captive fireflies, but something was different: the whole gallery was perfumed with a delicious smell, and the ants who lined the walls all seemed transfixed or drugged. The soldiers who had ushered them into the throne room fell back with dreamy looks upon their faces. They swayed gently, their four legs hanging limply at their sides.

"Which is Hormigüe?" Juna whispered.

Hercules could barely make out the queen. She was closely

crowded by scores of ants, all clinging like black beads to her throne. When she saw the humans, she stood and pushed the others away. Hercules gasped. The throne she sat on was more magnificent than ever. It was a pale, fresh yellow, and gave off the exquisite smell of the recent memory of honey.

"You!" she cried. "Did you really think you could deceive me? My hunters have informed me that the creature who accompanied you was a mouse. What, did you think you could spy on me in some futile attempt to outwit my allies the rats? You shall pay for your ungrateful behavior. My hunters are following the mouse's tracks at this moment. Soon they will find his city, and I shall be glad to hear of its destruction."

Beside him, Hercules could feel Juna seethe with anger, but he tried to keep his composure in the interests of diplomacy.

"My companion was no mouse," he lied boldly. "The one who accompanied me on our last visit was a human, this human beside me, in a transformed shape. We have found Kitty Joas, who restored my companion to her usual form, and now we return as we promised to tell you of the Tugot, for we are humans of our word."

"Human?" Hormigüe asked suspiciously. "Do you mean the Feet? But the Feet are giants, and you are so small a rat could crush you in its jaws."

"Small by magic, not by nature," Juna broke in. "We are indeed the Feet, with human skills and human knowledge. Do not underestimate us by our size. If we chose, we could crush a city of ants with a single footstep. But we do not so choose—we bring a gift instead."

Hercules sensed this was not the best line to take with Hormigüe, and he stepped on Juna's foot to silence her.

"As I was saying," he went on quickly, "now that my companion has her human shape once more, we are leaving to return to the world Outside the Walls. But we have been so impressed by you and your dominions—so much greater and more beautiful than anything else we have seen within the walls—that we wanted to help increase its glories."

"Yes?" asked Hormigüe. She seemed flattered, but Hercules could still hear the edge of suspicion in her voice.

"You have light and your light is lovely, but it is so uncertain. You said so yourself at our last meeting. It is a shame you do not have better illumination to shine on the masterworks of your people."

Hormigüe drew herself up and seemed even prouder than usual under Hercules' praise.

"We can help you," Juna broke in again. "In our travels, we have discovered a light so beautiful it rivals the sun that burns Outside the Walls. It is the magic of mice. We can be emissaries between you. Would you consider refusing to build the tunnel for the rats in exchange for such a prize?"

Hormigüe drew herself up even further. Her long, sparkling wings spread out slightly, like stiff, embroidered cloth or like a mantle made of leaded glass.

"Do I look like a common trader or merchant? Why should I trade when I can take? If this mouse light is so lovely, I will have the rats bring it back to us. We have the bronze lamp of the mice—perhaps we should have their light, as well."

"Their light will not work without fuel," Juna Loch interrupted, changing her tactics and her tone. "And the mice are willing to supply that fuel, if they could put themselves under your protection—"

"Silence!" Hormigüe barked. Juna's voice died in her throat. "The rats are our allies; the mice are nothing. I will not break the ancient contract. If the mice are useful as allies, they will be more useful still as slaves. I will help capture them, and they will show me their magic. If it pleases me, they will work to provide me with fuel. For you are right. I grow tired of the light of these inferior creatures." As she spoke, another firefly gave an agonized wail and its light fizzled out. The lamp-lighting ants came forward and opened the cage at the end of the taper, and the corpse fell to the ground with a tiny thud.

"And now," Hormigüe went on, "you may be the Feet, but it is more important that you have hands and can do work. I hope you will be useful to me, since you are decidedly not ornamental." She smiled down on Juna Loch. "You should have kept your mouse form, my dear," she said with a poisonous sweetness. "It was an improvement."

If she thought she was going to get a rise out of Juna, she was very much mistaken. "It is a fact that I like to be useful," Juna stated proudly. "I find it more admirable than sitting around looking pretty and behaving poorly. Nevertheless, I draw the line at being useful to tyrants—one must have some standards, after all."

Hormigüe's wings drooped for a fraction of a moment, and then she clapped her middle feet together. The servants struggled to come to attention against the hypnotizing smell of the honeyed throne.

"Take these creatures to the dairy," Hormigüe ordered, "and teach them to milk the aphids." She turned her back to them (showing those lovely wings, the wings that sparkled like veined diamonds) and settled herself again upon the throne.

Hercules and Juna felt themselves shoved along a passageway, hemmed in front and back by ants.

"Orrysay," Juna Loch said over the martial sound of the marching ants. "Iway inkthay Iway aymay avehay ewedscray everythingway upway."

"What?" Hercules asked impatiently. "You know, Juna, we don't have to speak pig Latin. They don't understand English."

"Oh, right!" Juna answered. "Good point! Listen, Herc, I'm sorry. You were doing great there. I should've just shut up. I need Kitty Joas just to save me from myself, I swear."

"Don't worry about it," Hercules said. "But now what?"

"The aforementioned Kitty Joas, I think. Maybe she can help us escape—or, at the very least, we can try to save the fireflies."

"Kitty Joas!" Hercules objected. "This isn't the way to her gates—this is the way to ant prison."

"As I understand it," Juna said, stopping short and smacking at the ants that were prodding her forward, "we don't really need to *get* anywhere to see her. Isn't that right? Isn't she upstairs, downstairs, and in my lady's chamber? How do we get her attention?"

"Quangster counted, but she said that this time we'd just have to call."

"Kitty Joas!" Juna called loudly. "Kitty Joas! We want to see you!" The ants looked at one another in confusion and backed slowly away, as if Juna Loch were dangerous.

It happened so quickly, Hercules didn't have time to warn her. Just as before, the walls melted away and the darkness was replaced with light, but this time Hercules felt himself falling with a splash into icy water. Little silver bubbles flew by his face, but just as he had figured out that he was drowning, he felt a strong hand grip his shirt and yank him to the surface. When his head broke above the water, he saw they were in the middle of a lake, a hundred feet from shore. Juna Loch was treading water beside him, holding on to his shirt to keep him from sinking back under. Her glasses were fogged, and her thin hair was plastered to her head, showing quite a lot of scalp.

"I *told* you fairies have a terrible sense of humor. Can you swim?"

"No." As he said it, he began to flail and sink.

"Just keep your face up, then," she said, "and *don't* grab around my neck. Drowning people always go for the neck, I swear. Very counterproductive. Stop thrashing, Hercules Amsterdam. I'll get you out. Don't you worry." She flipped on her side and began to swim a modified sidestroke, holding on to Hercules with one arm and paddling with the other, while her short strong legs kicked away. Hercules stared up at Kitty Joas' sky. He felt, suddenly, that his life was very strange.

"I will admit," Juna said to Hercules, once they were safely onshore, "I was not prepared for a dive into the drink when I packed for a trip within the walls. I—"

"So this is how you used your juminy juminy," a sweet voice called out. Hercules looked down the beach and saw the Tugot advancing under the swaying shade of a large green silk umbrella.

"This is my friend Juna Loch, my lady," he said uncertainly. "She has wanted very much to see the wonders of your land."

"She is seeing them," Kitty Joas replied. "Not many visitors see what she has seen. My lake is filled with extraordinary fish that few have ever witnessed."

"It is also extraordinarily cold," Juna said flatly. "I might even say it is coldness itself. Have you got such a thing as a towel about?"

Kitty Joas waved her paw, and they found that they were dry.

"That," said Juna begrudgingly, "is a fine trick, I swear."

"Yet you did not come here to see tricks," Kitty Joas said to Juna, fixing her with her steely glance. "You came instead to give me your opinion. You do not approve of me, Ermengarde Ashland. But now you are here. Speak, child, though I will not promise to answer."

Juna stared at Kitty Joas suspiciously. "I have many questions," she said. "How is it that you just happened to be wherever Hercules was, both times he wanted to see you?"

"I wasn't," answered Kitty Joas.

"Did you just hurry here, then, when you saw us fall into the lake?"

"I was in my northern palace, two days away, when I heard you call," Kitty Joas said. "I walked here at my leisure and opened the gate. When Hercules called before, I was in my own library. Again, I went at my own pace to join him. If it seemed instantaneous to you, it is only because your time does not pass as my time passes."

"Oh, right," said Juna Loch.

"But that is not what is bothering you," Kitty Joas stated.

"No, in point of fact it is not," Juna Loch responded, with a defiant tone in her voice that Hercules worried was dangerous when addressing a Tugot. "It is your way of dishing out your favors that bothers me. Why not just help people, you know, out of the goodness of your heart?"

"That is not the way a Tugot's magic works," Kitty Joas answered. "At least that is not the way my magic works, and I am the only Tugot I know."

"What did you take from Hercules, then?"

"What he values most—his smallness."

"I didn't give *that* up," Hercules burst in. "I'm still small now, and I'm staying small. I won't ever use the last juminy juminy."

"Of course not," Kitty Joas said pleasantly. She turned back to Juna Loch and looked her up and down. "But *you* . . . I could do so much for you. I could make you beautiful, if you like. I could straighten your nose, make your hair that red color I know you secretly desire, perfect your vision, make you slender—"

"And if I were interested," Juna Loch interrupted, "what would you make me give up?"

"Simply your ugliness," Kitty Joas replied.

"Then I will keep it," Juna answered triumphantly. "You said yourself that you would only take a thing of value—maybe someday I will find out why my ugliness is so important to me." She took a long significant look at Kitty Joas' perfect form, at her glossy black fur and silky tail. Then she gave the Tugot a crooked smile of reconciliation, but Hercules could detect more than a trace of triumph in it. "But perhaps I will ask for your help—that is, if I may ask on someone else's behalf?"

"Few make that choice, but it is possible."

"And would you ask *me* to pay for it, or would it be that someone else who would have to give something up?"

Kitty Joas smiled. "You *will* give me something you treasure before you leave my lands, but I will not keep it long."

Juna looked concerned for a moment, but then she went

on, "Well then, I ask you on behalf of Hormigüe, the queen of the ants. She needs help in turning honeydew into light so that the fireflies can be freed. Can you bring her here and do it?"

"Of course I can do it," Kitty Joas retorted. "You forget to whom you talk."

"I just meant to ask if Hercules and I could avoid going back to see her. We're not really in a hurry to be back in her anty clutches anytime soon, let me tell you. Would you mind if we just snuck out the back way?" She smiled hopefully.

But Kitty Joas merely yawned. "I tire of having mortals in my lands," she said. "And I have no desire to have you wandering about unsupervised. You will come with me."

"Oh, well," Juna said to Hercules. "I tried."

"It's not that far to Hormigüe's," Hercules called out, trying to cover up Juna's rudeness.

"In your time, perhaps," Kitty Joas replied. "But you may have noticed that we are in a little valley here. Even to get around a corner of your world we have to cross one of those mountains." And she waved her paw at an impressive peak that towered above them.

"I *knew* we should have had a bigger snack at your house," Juna muttered.

"You may pick some oona fruit, if you wish," Kitty Joas told her, pulling down the branches of one of the trees. Golden berries grew in thick bunches among the dark green leaves, and Juna picked one dubiously. She took a small bite and the suspicion was wiped from her face as if washed off with a sponge. She ate handful after handful hungrily. "You've got to try this, I swear," she said to Hercules with her mouth full. But before

Hercules could pluck some from the branch, Juna suddenly clutched her throat. Her tongue and lips moved, but no sound came out.

"What did you do to her?" Hercules demanded.

"Oh, nothing," Kitty Joas replied. "Oona fruit is quite delicious, of course, but it temporarily robs anyone who eats it of the power of speech." Hercules wasn't quite sure, but he thought he saw a hint of a smile touch Kitty Joas' delicate mouth. He was quite certain that he saw Juna Loch mouthing, "I *told* you fairies have a terrible sense of humor."

It was a quiet journey.

Kitty Joas led the way over the rocky paths of the mountain, but before long she stopped them. "This can be a tedious way to travel when one has other business," she said, "and I have much other business. I cannot always be acting on the whims of those who should not even be within my walls." She waved her hands, and the earth beneath them seemed suddenly to wiggle and waver. It rose up into the air like a flying carpet, moving at an alarming speed. In a heart-stopping moment, they were on top of the mountain. Kitty Joas put up one hand then, and the great vista before them melted into the green-lit gallery of the ant queen. When Hormigüe saw Kitty Joas, her antennae stood straight up.

"Hormigüe!" the Tugot called. "Daughter of Formique and heir to the throne of Hormiga-Ra, it is I, Kitty Joas."

"You are real!" Hormigüe cried, falling from her throne to one knee. In her agitation, her cap of butterfly scales came loose and fell over one eye.

"I am real," Kitty Joas repeated, "and I am here. These humans suggest that I give you what you have not. Shall I teach you a magic? Shall I teach you how to make light from honey-dew?"

Hormigüe hesitated. Then she bowed low (all the while making sure Kitty Joas could see her magnificent wings) and crossed her four legs in front of her chest. "The Feet are right, your Tugotic majesty," she said almost humbly. "I deserve the best light within the walls. Teach me, Kitty Joas. It shall add to my glory that you have shared your magic with us."

"I always require something for my favors," Kitty Joas said. "In return for this magic, will you send your fireflies away?"

"It is already done, your greatness," Hormigüe assented.

"Then," Kitty Joas said, turning to Hercules and Juna Loch, "you may go. This magic is not for your eyes."

Juna and Hercules moved quickly to the door, but Hormigüe's voice rang out, "Do not forget that you are my prisoners! Take them!" Hercules looked at Juna in despair. He had hoped that Hormigüe would change her mind about imprisoning them, but now he found himself once more herded toward the dairy by a company of ants. Hercules waited for Juna to say something ironic but she, of course, was silent. She did not even make a move to escape as the ants pushed them deeper and deeper into the colony.

It was not until they had passed the storerooms and drawn near the great paddocks that held the aphids that Hercules saw her reach for her belt. Her hand found one of the pouches and opened it stealthily before removing a plastic container. All the guard ants suddenly stopped. Juna raised the container over her head. It was full of something dark that glittered. Then she threw it as hard as she could down the passage behind them. It was not a very good throw, but it did the trick. The ants all ran after it like dogs after a bone, and Juna grabbed Hercules' hand and pulled him away from their captors. The passage grew lighter and lighter as they ran, and in a moment Hercules could see an ant hole that seemed to lead outside the walls. Juna pushed Hercules through and tried to squeeze through it herself. It was a very tight fit, and the belt made it tighter. Juna grew red in the face as she tried to wiggle through, and tears came to her eyes as Hercules yanked at her arms, but finally she made it. They were in the basement of Hercules' house. He recognized the clank and whine of the washing machine.

"What was *that?*" he panted.

"Any," she mouthed.

"Any?" he repeated.

Juna rolled her eyes. She dug in a pouch for the notebook and a pen. *Honey,* she wrote.

"Honey?" Hercules repeated dumbly, and then he understood. "Oh, I get it," he said. "I can't believe you remembered about ants and honey."

I thought of it when you first mentioned it to me, Juna wrote. *I like to be prepared.*

"And I'm grateful for it," Hercules said. "But now what?"

Now we find that pipe again.

"The pipe?"

Yes, the pipe—that smelly pipe. Weren't you just about to realize that it was the pipe to the rats when we were taken captive by the ants? she wrote.

"Was I?" Hercules asked. "I've kind of forgotten. Do we really have to?"

Oh, yes, she wrote. *It's our only hope.*

"Because I was actually hoping we wouldn't have to," Hercules said. "It seems very . . . *unsanitary* to go down a sewer pipe."

Buck up, Hercules! she wrote. *It's bound to be interesting. Come on, let's go on to the next chapter of our adventure.*

And so they did.

IT DIDN'T TAKE THEM LONG to find the pipe again. As Hercules told Juna, the basement they were in had once contained a darkroom. The door had swollen after a springtime flooding and would no longer close properly, but nobody had much cared. There had often been a terrible smell there anyway.

"The pipe must be behind the darkroom wall," Hercules reasoned. "Maybe we can get back to the pipe through there."

The warped door was slightly ajar, but it still took all their strength to pull it open wide enough for them to squeeze through. The room was dim and horribly dusty, a kind of mossy dust piled here and there in misshapen forms, reminding Hercules of Kitty Joas' topiary garden. The light fixture had fallen from the ceiling close to the floor, and Juna turned it on by pulling with all her might on the little beaded cord. When the light came on, Hercules rather wished it hadn't; it was a red photographer's lamp that lit the room with an eerie glow. In the back of the room, they could see a gaping hole a plumber had once made in the wall behind the sink. In a moment, they were back within the walls, standing before the malodorous opening of the pipe, peering down into the sewer below.

"Hey—I was right!" Hercules said, but his excitement paled when he noticed a set of footprints in the dust. Hercules measured his own foot against the clawed marks and shivered. "They're so *big*," he said in a small voice. Juna nodded absently. She was scribbling furiously in her little notebook.

"Maybe this is a bad idea," Hercules said, looking longingly toward the safety of the darkroom. "No, not maybe—I *know* this is a bad idea. Don't you see, Juna, there was a *rat* walking around here? Did you see the size of his foot? I don't think we want to be here when he comes back, and I certainly don't want to be down *there* in the pipe. . . ."

Juna ripped the piece of paper out of her notebook and thrust it at Hercules.

It'll be fine—a grand adventure.

"Yeah, right," Hercules said. He read on.

We don't want to engage the enemy—we just want to lay low and listen. Remember, darkness and silence will be our cloak of invisibility. No flashlights! No talking! No rustling, no scratching, no sneezing! And remember! All for one and one for all behind enemy lines.

"Do you at least have anything in that belt to protect us with?" Hercules asked.

Don't worry. I like to be prepared.

"How do we get down?"

It's duck tape for us, Hercarino.

"Duck tape?" Hercules sputtered. "*Duck tape?* How's that going to help?" But Juna had already removed the silvery duct tape from her belt. She grabbed his hand and began wrapping great wads of it, sticky side out, around his palms. He stared at her in amazement.

She picked up the notebook again and wrote. *Don't worry. It'll hold us. Just keep unwinding it if it loses its stickiness.* Then she wrapped up her own hands and mouthed, "Let's go."

"I *really* don't like this," Hercules said, but Juna very calmly slipped into the pipe and placed her sticky hands on its walls.

"Is it easy?" Hercules whispered after her hopefully. The top of Juna's head shook back and forth, no. Hercules sighed and lowered himself over the edge.

Juna was making her slow way down the pipe, but Hercules could not move. He found himself dangling there, sticky hands pressed to the wall and his legs kicking uselessly below him. Finally, tentatively, he pulled a hand free and pressed it down again a little lower on the pipe. It held. He tried again. It was working! He was doing it! He was climbing down a sewer pipe with the help of duct tape! Despite the slight ache in his arms, he began to enjoy the rhythm of his descent: *rrrip* (went the tape pulling free from the wall), *thump* (went the tape, sticking to the wall), *humph* (went Hercules, drawing in a deep breath), *rrrip* (went the first hand), *thump* (went the other), *hooph* (went Hercules, letting out a deep breath), *rrrip, thump, humph, rrrip, thump, hooph, rrrip, thump, humph, rrrip, AAAAH!* (went Hercules, falling unknown feet down the pipe, smashing into Juna halfway down, and the two of them crashing onto the floor at the bottom).

He lay still for a moment, feebly trying to catch his breath. He was so confused by his sudden fall that it didn't occur to him to get off Juna until she gave him a push. In the darkness, he could hear her puffing beside him. He imagined her mouthing words at him: "Hercules Amsterdam, I swear. When you fall down a pipe on top of a lady, you don't just lie there. Did you forget to pull back the tape to keep it sticky? I bet you did. My lord." He was glad for the dimness.

"Are you okay?" he whispered. She whacked him on the arm. "Oh, right," he whispered. "Quiet." She whacked him again, then pulled him to his feet. He stood up straight and smacked his head on what seemed to be a very low ceiling; he fell down again. In the darkness he could just make out that the pipe made a sharp turn and ran off horizontally into the fetid unknown.

Juna was already creeping along the pipe. Hercules followed close behind, keeping one hand on her useful belt, the other pressed over his face. The stench was overwhelming: rank, foul, putrid, noisome, nasty. It was the smell of garbage piled high on the streets on trash day—the smell of rotten meat, old eggs, and soured milk, all mixed together with a miasma of dirty diapers. Juna stopped him then and tied a bandanna around his nose and mouth, covering the stench with the pleasant smell of her laundry detergent. "I'm glad you like to be prepared," he whispered. She whacked him again.

It was not too long before the pipe widened out into a little cavern. As they kept close to the walls, Hercules had the impression that they were walking on old, damp newspapers, or perhaps something even more disgusting. The floor grew increasingly thick with garbage, the walking increasingly treacherous. Once Hercules slipped on what might have been a whole rotting banana peel, and soon afterward Juna tripped facedown into a yogurt container. They continued, sliding and tripping, trodding and slipping, until they were both covered with garbage and smelled no better than the rest of the pipe. *At least it's covering* our *smell,* Hercules thought as he slipped again. It all would have been very comical, he felt, if it hadn't been so very disgusting, and it would have been merely disgusting if it hadn't been for the disturbing sounds directly ahead of them.

In front of them they could see the dull burning red of smudge fires, and Hercules suspected that the rats were burning garbage. It was fitting, he felt, for all creatures within the walls seemed to burn what they loved most. They crept forward toward the light and suddenly found themselves at the edge of a great room. They could just make out the piles of burning garbage—the rats did not bother with making lamps—and in the firelight they saw the shapes of their enemies lolling about and gnawing on bones.

Up close the rats were grotesquely large—some more than three times Hercules' height. They slobbered and they spit, and when they talked in their crude, coarse version of the common tongue, their speech seemed not only ugly but uninteresting. For the first time, Hercules felt his terror of the rats colored by disgust. They were not just evil, he felt, but repulsive and despicable. Strangely, it made him braver.

He was so overwhelmed with disgust and superiority that without a moment's thought he started to walk right up to them, to tell them to their dirty faces just what he thought of them, when Juna Loch pulled him back. Suddenly he was swept with an icy fear. What had he been thinking? The rats were revolting and they were gross; they were probably as stupid as they appeared, but they were still at least twice his size and they were armed, if not with brains, then with fearsome teeth and claws. He began to shake. He might even have been detected then if it hadn't been for Juna, who pulled him behind a pile of apples heaped up in a corner.

It would have been the perfect hiding place, except that many of the apples were soft and old, and they seemed as big as boulders to Hercules. As they climbed the great pile, Hercules' leg sank up to the hip into a rotten place, and he lost his balance. When he grasped a stem to try to steady himself, another apple slipped on top of Juna. For the first time, he was glad that she had lost her voice.

Once they were fully hidden behind the apples, Hercules looked over at Juna. She seemed fine, but the apple had knocked one of the lenses out of her glasses. She was calmly fixing them, using a small screwdriver from a little kit in her belt. When she saw Hercules looking at her, she rubbed her head where the apple had hit and smiled wryly. There was something so comical and comforting in her crooked smile, even in this most perilous of adventures, that it made Hercules smile back.

While Juna was fixing her glasses, Hercules peered out of a little hole between two apples. He was just in time to see the beginning of a horrific melee. One rat, who was busily licking the blood from a rancid package of meat, was suddenly attacked by another. In an instant, rat squeals and screams filled the hall, and when Hercules saw them fight—saw the teeth and claws in action and the foaming blood that splattered the walls—his courage froze. Juna pressed beside him and the two watched in horror.

The first rat did not take long to finish off his opponent. He took the throat of the other between his teeth and shook him hard; Hercules could hear the neck snap. The victor launched into a long and tedious song about his valor.

Hercules might have been thoroughly sick then if they had not been suprised by the cacophonous racket coming from the darkness. Juna rapped Hercules hard on the arm. Something was coming into the chamber, something that moved like Kitty Joas' flying carpet. It looked feathery and elegant, until they could see what it was. Hercules felt Juna shiver beside him. It was centipedes—hundreds of them. Several rats walked behind them, playing on discordant instruments made of bone and what looked like whiskers. As one passed by him, Hercules could see that bits of meat and gristle still clung to the bones they used as flutes. After the musicians came a score of earwigs hauling on ropes that creaked and groaned as they pulled a grotesque structure into view. As it approached, it appeared even more hideous. It was a huge pile of rat-sized skulls, somehow cemented together in a monstrous jumble. The rat king rode upon it. He wore a crown of stag beetles on his head, and in his hand he carried a scepter. It was made of a long leg bone of some small animal, topped with three skulls so tiny that Hercules could only guess they had come from mice.

"I see my son Ukpat is dead," he observed, looking down at the body of the rat. "Who killed him?"

The killer stood up, his paw placed proudly on his heart. "I killed him, Father, in glorious battle."

"Very well, Ukpit, my son," the king approved. "I congratulate you on your kill. My crown may well be yours someday." He lolled on his loathsome throne as the centipede carpet that had preceded him fanned out around the room. The earwigs made a circle around him, opening and shutting their sharp pincers.

"I have always assumed I will be king," said the smaller rat. "I will kill you before too long, my father."

The rat king smiled affectionately. "Or I, you," he said. "For I am still strong, and the strongest shall rule. Might makes right, my son, as you have been taught. The only justice is strength. Kill me if you can, and may you reign for many generations before you in turn are killed by your own son."

"Or a daughter," one of the other rats guffawed. Ukpit ran at him, and they scuffled bloodily. The king put up his hand, and both rats stopped.

"To acknowledge such insults is beneath you, Ukpit. You are strong. You know and I know that only a male could kill you. That piece of *iskit* insults you only because he knows he will die at the hand of a female himself."

Beside him, Hercules could see Juna clench her hands in indignation, and her eyes flashed.

The king stood up from his throne; the centipedes flocked back to surround him. Slowly (for he was old and fat), he stepped down from the great pile of skulls. For all his boasting, he seemed bloated and weak. Only his voice rang with royalty. The carpet of centipedes and earwigs undulated around him.

"There is one task before you, my son, before we battle for the throne. Not all are worthy to rule. It has always been that a rat must prove himself before he is accepted as king. He must show himself free of mercy and free of fear and create a double symbol of his rule—a scepter proving his victory over both the weak and the strong. Look upon it!" He brandished the scepter above his head. "Here are the skulls of the weak, the skulls of mice. And here is the leg bone of the strong, of our last king, my father. Someday it may be you who takes my bone for your scepter, Ukpit. But you must collect your skulls before we can battle to the death."

He turned from his son then and looked out over the rest of the crowd before his voice rang out again. "The time is nigh!" he called. "Soon you will all be able to collect your skulls! The females have done their work. The throne has been delivered, and our servants the ants now track the mice. Soon the messengers will come. Are you ready?" The rats nodded. "I asked, are you ready?"

"We are ready!" they cried in a single voice. "We are rats! We thirst for the blood of the weak!"

Suddenly, Hercules felt Juna stiffen beside him. When he glanced at her face, he could see that she was in an agony of anticipation and fear. Her wide-eyed expression and the finger pressed underneath her nose told Hercules that she was going to sneeze. It could not be at a worse time. The rat king was not six inches from the pile of apples.

When the sneeze came, it was tremendous. It nearly knocked Hercules over. The two of them crouched together in terror, but nothing happened: no rats peered over the edge of the pile; no claws dragged them into the dim light. Slowly, the fear uncoiled from their hearts, and they breathed normally once more. The rats had not heard. The sneeze had been silent: Juna's voice was still lost. Hercules was flooded with sweet relief.

On the other side of the apples, the rat king continued. "There is one danger," he said, his voice dropping to a low pitch. "There are always those soldiers who find themselves pitying the mice. They look so much like our own ratlings, so small, so defenseless." His voice grew quiet and almost tender, as if he were smiling indulgently upon his own little babes. Then he raised his voice to a furious growl. "Do not make this mistake! Too often I have seen warriors turn to women in battle. Purge your hearts of pity! Purge your hearts of tenderness! Weakness means wrong! Might makes right!"

He walked among the rats, looking like a schoolmaster in a boys' school, his paws clasped behind his back.

"And who is stronger than a rat?" he asked, in a low, reasonable tone. "Only the enemy whose name is too terrible to mention. And in the end, we are even stronger than that enemy, for we can bring down its human master. The Legs flee from our name. Again and again we have triumphed over them, bringing the Black Death to their doors. And we shall do it again. The Plague Rat has returned. Soon he will share his weapons with us all and spread death among the Legs as we spread death among the mice. For we are Rats! We are mighty, and might makes right! Say it, my sons! Shout it! Sing it! Sing it, my sons, with all your hearts!"

"Might makes right! Might makes right!" the rats chanted like creatures possessed. Then Hercules saw a terrible sight. The pile of apples was suddenly covered with centipedes, oozing over the top of the heap and falling over. They rushed over the rotten fruit and then over Juna Loch, who was standing, petrified, as one curled around her neck like a hideous feather boa.

It was at this moment that they discovered Juna's voice had returned.

Her scream rang out like a shot. They looked at each other in terror, and together tried desperately to clamber over the slippery apples. The pile wobbled, the apples rolled, and Hercules and Juna tumbled out at the very feet of the rat king. Numbly, Hercules looked up at the cruel face looming above him. For a moment, it seemed as if time had frozen as he stared into the rat's beady eyes. Hercules' blood pounded in his ears. Then the rat king's surprise was transformed into loathing. He raised his clawed fist, and Hercules braced himself for the blow. But suddenly Juna hurled something into the face of the king, and the room filled with a dense smoke and a sickly floral odor. In the confusion, Juna grabbed Hercules' hand and pulled him toward the pipe back into the house.

"What was that?" Hercules panted.

"Perfume bomb," Juna answered. "I didn't know if it would work—it is a device of my own invention, though I never thought I would use it under these circumstances."

They continued running through the pipe, slipping and sliding on the bits of rotten apple that covered their shoes. Before too long, they had reached the elbow where the pipe turned upward in Hercules' house. They could just make out the dim red light from the darkroom above.

"All right," Hercules said, looking expectantly at Juna's belt. "How do we get back up the pipe?"

"I don't know," she said distractedly. "I'm out of duck tape."

"What?" Hercules shrieked. "Juna, *how are we going to get up?*"

"Don't ask me yet," she said. "I'm thinking. Don't panic."

"Oh, no," Hercules moaned, wrapping his arms around himself and panicking anyway. "We need help, we really do, this is the time we really need help. . . . Kitty Joas! Kitty Joas! Your children need you! Please, Kitty Joas! Open your gates!"

Juna put up a finger as she thought. The sound of the distant commotion was coming closer; they could make out individual voices.

"You hear that?" Hercules groaned. "They're looking for us! Juna, is *now* the time I can ask you how we're going to get up?"

For the first time since he had met her, Juna Loch seemed to be at a loss. She touched each of the little leather pouches in turn, thinking about their contents, and then she turned to Hercules with an unhappy look on her face. She opened her mouth, closed it, and gave him a miserable shrug.

It was then that the miraculous thing happened. As they stood there, staring hopelessly up that infinitely long pipe, their tired eyes saw a faint glow, a glow that swirled and swooped down lower toward them.

"It's Kitty Joas!" Hercules cried wildly. "She's coming! She's coming!"

The glow came closer. Hercules could hear a buzzing melody, and then they were surrounded by dozens—scores—hundreds of little lights. It was the fireflies.

"Juna Loch! Juna Loch!" they called in their tiny voices. "We have been searching for you since your words freed us from the ant queen. When you were a little girl and lay in the grass and watched us, we marked your kindness. Yet none of us could imagine that you would save us in our darkest hour. Juna Loch! Juna Loch! We are here to save you as you have saved us. What shall we do for you?"

A smile broke across Juna's face, and she opened her arms to embrace the swarm of insects. After half a second's thought, she pulled the rope off her belt and handed it to the fireflies. "Can you pull us up?" she asked.

The great swarm buzzed and hummed and flashed to one another, and then, grabbing the edges of the rope, they wove in and out in coordinated complexity and produced a small hammock, just wide enough for Juna Loch with Hercules on her lap. Grabbing the rope's ends, the swarm rose up the pipe, with Hercules and Juna swaying pleasantly under the gorgeous flashing iridescence of uncountable fireflies.

15

"I DIDN'T THINK we were going to make it," Hercules said after the fireflies had dropped them at the top of the pipe and flown flashing away. He pressed his hand to his racing heart. Juna was taking a quick inventory of the remaining items in her belt. Then she cocked her head and listened. "Shhh!" she hissed, and Hercules heard it—the sound of scratching and breathing that came up out of the pipe.

"At this juncture," Juna Loch whispered, "it is my considered opinion that we run."

And so they ran—Hercules to the left, Juna to the right, then both right at each other, and finally (a little dazed and bruised) down the passageway together.

"Not this way!" Juna suddenly shouted. "Let's get back outside!"

But as they turned around, they could see the hulking silhouette of a rat between them and the red light of the darkroom. They were trapped within the walls.

"Over here!" Juna called. "Go for the pipes!" They headed for a forest of pipes—thin copper water pipes that rose like redwood trees to the upper stories of the house and thick iron outlet pipes like the trunks of immense sequoias. They squeezed behind them where no rat could follow, then ran.

They kept going for a long time in the blackness. Suddenly the passage grew soft and slippery, like soap or ash under their feet. Juna switched on her flashlight for a brief moment—they were back in Ulrich's city.

"This way," Hercules whispered, pointing to the paths that switchbacked upward from terrace to terrace. Using the flashlight so they wouldn't tumble off the terraced heights, they raced up the abandoned mouseways to the upper levels of the city, nearly falling several times where the road had been destroyed. They were almost to the baseball field when a rat jumped out at them.

"You're trapped," he said in his growled version of the common speech.

"We're trapped!" Hercules wailed. In petrified fascination, he looked into the rat's eyes, which shone with sadistic pleasure.

Suddenly Hercules' fear boiled away under the force of his anger and disgust. "Juna!" he commanded. "The pepper!"

Juna opened a pouch of her belt and threw a black handful at the rat, who shrieked and scuttled away from them, his paws to his eyes. He took one step too many and fell with a squeal and a muffled thud to the bottom of Ulrich's city. "Good thinking," Juna panted. Then she took him by the arm and began to run again.

In the darkness behind them, they could hear another rat

following. Juna gave a little squeak. Hercules looked down and saw the shadow moving toward them; he looked up at the path switchbacking above them; and then he looked across the chasm to the opposite side of the city. The wire bridge was still there, connecting the two sides of the cavern—and Hercules knew what they had to do.

"Come on!" he yelled to Juna, heading for the bridge. The destroyed city square was far below him, but somehow he felt no fear.

"Are you crazy, Hercules Amsterdam? We can't cross *that!*"

But Hercules had already stepped out onto it. He wobbled a little, but then Sangster's voice whispered in his ear and steadied him. He was doing it! He was crossing the wire like a tightrope walker! His feet seemed to grip the wire as easily as if they were mouse paws.

"It's okay!" he called back to Juna. "Just don't look down!"

"I'm looking down!" he heard her moan.

But Hercules made it to the other side, and he turned and called back encouragingly, "That's it, Juna. Put your arms out. Don't worry—"

She was not halfway across when the rat appeared at the edge of the terrace. He tentatively put a clawed foot on the bridge and stopped.

"Should I come eat you, or wait for you to fall, little weakling?" the rat mocked. Juna whimpered.

"Come on, Juna! You can do it!" Hercules urged. "Don't let that rat scare you! Move your feet!"

Juna wavered and panicked, but she was almost across. Hercules reached out his hand to help her over the last few inches.

On the other side of the chasm, the rat snarled and steadied its foot on the wire. Almost without thinking, Hercules reached out and fumbled with the bulging pockets of Juna's belt. Snatching up a pair of wire cutters, he bent down to the bridge. The wire snapped and fell, stranding the rat on the other side of the cavern. The rat began to swear. But Juna and Hercules were running again, and its words were lost in the gloom of Ulrich's city.

"How did you know I'd have wire cutters?" Juna wheezed as they ran.

"I knew you like to be prepared," Hercules answered.

When they had passed into the blank spaces between the walls, they stopped for Juna to use her inhaler. "Okay, that's better," she said. "Tell me, are there paths all through the walls?"

"Some," Hercules answered, "but mostly it's just blank spaces, wires, or pipes—except where the cities are."

"Let's stay away from the paths, then. It'll be harder for the rats to follow."

"But where are we going?" Hercules asked Juna's back as she pushed aside the wires like creepers in a jungle, looking for the best one to climb up.

"Up and out," she said. "It seems ill-advised to go back the way we came and run into more rats, and I don't want to lead them to the mouse city. Up and out is the way to go."

"I get *up*," Hercules said, "but *out* . . . ?"

"I'm of a gambling nature," Juna answered enigmatically. Then she sighed. "Oh, *no*," she said.

Hercules heard it, too—the unnerving sound of the rats in pursuit, speeding along on their clawed feet.

"Okay," Juna said, "time for up." She grabbed one of the wires and began hauling herself up, hand over fist. Hercules followed. When the wires ended, they swung themselves up onto the broad beams of the next floor and raced across them looking for other wires. Then they were shimmying up again. Hercules panted and Juna wheezed, but the sound of the rats was farther away now, and a soft glow appeared above them.

Finally Juna stopped Hercules on a beam. "We're here," she said. "We just have to push through *that*," and she pointed at some pink fiberglass insulation. Together, they struggled through it, pushing at the plaster and lath on the other side until they could break through. Then they both fell, panting, onto the attic floor.

Hercules breathed a sigh of relief. There were no terrifying sounds here. There was only the creak of the tall trees and the breeze coming through the open window, and an unearthly cooing coming from under the eaves. The sun was streaming in through a cracked window, and the room smelled of warm wood. In exhaustion, Hercules lay on the splash of sunlight on the floor, but Juna had opened her belt once more. She was crumbling up the cookies she had brought as a snack and was sprinkling the crumbs everywhere.

"What are you doing?"

"An offering," she whispered.

It was at that moment that two things happened at once. To Hercules' left, a rat burst through the insulation in the wall and stood before them in greedy triumph. To Hercules' right, something big and gray suddenly flew into view and pecked at the crumbs. "Hurry!" Juna shouted, and, before the surprised rat could react, Juna and Hercules grabbed on to the pigeon's feet and were carried through the open window into the safety beyond.

16

FLYING WAS NOTHING like what Hercules had imagined, but then again, he had never imagined that his first experience of flight would be while dangling from the legs of a large pigeon. It was precarious at best. As the bird took off through the window, it folded its legs close to its body, as landing gear folds into an airplane, and Hercules thought his wrists would break. Then there was the constant beating of the wings that threatened to sweep Hercules off to his death, and the ground that rose up dizzily to meet them. But suddenly Hercules was rolling on the cool green grass in front of Juna's house, listening to Juna thank the pigeon profusely with many "I swear"s and "let me tell *you*"s.

Hercules could hardly manage a bow. Half of him was still expecting the rat's bite and the other was fighting a strong wave of nausea that seemed to come from relief. "Thank you," he managed finally. The pigeon fixed Hercules with one red eye and nodded with great dignity. Then he turned back to Juna Loch.

"Juna Loch," he cooed, "when you were a little girl, we watched you and marked your kindness. You never chased us, and it has been many a time that you have kept other children from rushing at us as we have gone about our small business. We thank you also for your gifts of food. It has been a debt too long uncompensated, but I hope I have done something to repay you." He bowed deeply, then took off with a great sweeping motion into the sky and back to his nest in the eaves.

"I can't believe we're safe," Hercules panted. "I thought we were rat chow, I swear."

Juna smiled and patted her belt. "Yes-siree-bob, that was a close call, and no mistake. But there's still much to do, Herco. No rest for the weary on their laurels, I always say, although a small snack might be in order. I think we'd better take some more juminy juminy, though, before we try to brave Princess in the kitchen."

They had just taken the juminy juminy, with barely enough time to shake out their newly large limbs, when Hercules heard a sound that made his stomach lurch.

"Here comes the charge of the dimwit brigade," Juna said calmly as the same boys Hercules had seen before rushed up to them on their bicycles, hooting and screaming. "Hey, shorty!" they called, and Hercules realized they meant him. His cheeks burned. He almost thought he was going to throw up.

The boys circled closer around them, like a tightening noose, and then they fell back, holding their noses.

"Did Mommy forget to give you a bath?" one of them taunted. Hercules suddenly realized that the sewer smell still clung to them, and he blushed even harder.

One of the others leaned forward and said sympathetically, "No wonder you have to find your friends at the dog pound, little boy."

The third had turned to Juna. "So you finally got yourself a boyfriend." He laughed. "Look at the dog and the scared little mouse! Just be sure she doesn't *eat* you, mouse-boy!" And he laughed so hard he almost fell down. Hercules' eyes burned; he thought he would almost rather be in the rats' pipe than have to face those boys. But Juna was unperturbed.

"Good afternoon," she said to the boys as she opened the door for Hercules. She bowed to them once and then followed Hercules into the house. She shut the door behind her and unbuckled the belt from about her waist and let it drop onto the back of the couch. She sat down beside the belt and patted it proudly. "My goodness, I love this belt," she said. When Hercules didn't respond, she looked at him severely.

"Hercules," she observed, "you're shaking."

"I—I—those boys—"

"Hercules," she reproved, "don't tell me that after having the courage to escape from carpenter-ant slavery, slide down a sewer pipe to the very stronghold of the enemy, not to mention survive a very close chase throughout the walls of the house, that you're bothered by some moronic little boys? I swear. Think about it!"

"I just don't like being teased," he said.

"Well, *duh*," she answered. She unfastened the swinging door into the kitchen and slipped inside, where she was greeted by Princess' hysterical barks. "I don't like mosquito bites, either, but it's best not to scratch them." She came back in a moment with a sizable tower of peanut-butter crackers on a tray. "So they tease you. My father says that if you're not interesting enough to get teased, you'll grow up to be boring. I bet those boys don't even know why they tease—they probably only do it to impress the rest of the morons. It's almost sad, isn't it? They'd be mighty friendly if it was just one of them and us on a desert island, I'd bet. But how sad, to be on a desert island with those idiots. They wouldn't even know how to make fire."

"*I* don't know how to make fire," Hercules said dejectedly.

"Sure, but you'd learn. Okay, maybe they'd learn, too. They just need to be separated from the pack and turned from rats to humans, you know?"

"I don't know," Hercules sighed. "I don't think I'll ever be able to ignore them."

"I tell you, it's just not worth your while to be bothered," Juna said. "We simply don't have the time. Now we know the rats are about to attack, and there's the Plague Rat, too. Oh, yes, we have work to do and then some, I swear."

"We didn't even learn the rats' weaknesses," Hercules said gloomily, still thinking about the boys.

"Well, in point of fact, we did," Juna argued. "They are arrogant, uncivilized, and sexist. Any of those weaknesses could be fatal. And they are overly proud—and pride goeth before destruction. It's just like them to think *they* spread the plague, when really their fleas do all the work, I swear. And besides, we learned that the rats have an enemy 'whose name is too terrible to mention.' Maybe we can figure out who that is. Come on, Hercules, eat something! No point wasting away, *I* always say."

They brainstormed with their mouths full. Juna's plans grew increasingly elaborate, and Hercules had to rein her in before electronics became involved.

"Why do we have to make it so complicated?" he complained. "Can't we just put bars over the pipe? Couldn't we just lock them up?"

"Sure," Juna said. From the tone of her voice, Hercules worried that she was about to launch into a disappointed objection, but then she started over in a more enthusiastic tone. "That's a fine idea, Herco. We can easily do that. Come on, I know just what to do." She sniffed her shirt delicately. "But perhaps the morons had a point. We should probably remove some of the *eau de* rat before we venture out into polite company."

After they took turns cleaning themselves up in Juna's bathroom, Juna led the way to the garage. Hercules followed, the borrowed clothing flapping around him as he walked. "I'm guessing you don't have a bike," Juna said, opening the garage door and wheeling her own bicycle out.

"Uh," Hercules replied, "I had a doll bike once, but the pedals kept sticking."

"No problem. You can sit on the back of my seat and I'll give you a ride. It's totally great, I tell you. But *don't* hold on around my throat. I like to use my throat for breathing, you know."

And it *was* great. Much better than clinging on to a pigeon's legs, and even better than riding on Kitty Joas' magic carpet. Hercules was quite enjoying being human-sized, especially when Juna decided that they should take ten minutes out of the hero business to eat ice cream—real, cold, creamy ice cream that made everything Hercules had ever eaten between the walls seem like reconstituted sawdust. Then Juna locked the bike to a stop sign and led the way into a hardware store.

"Hello, Albert!" she called from the door. "This is my new friend, Hercules. We've come to make use of your expertise." A broad smile passed over the clerk's face as he saw Juna. He laid the thick book he was reading down on the counter and stuck his hand out to Hercules.

"Hello, Hercules," he said, in an interested and friendly voice. "Hello, Juna. How did the bat house go? Did you get it up?"

"Of course I did," Juna said, offended. "I always finish my projects. But bats I have none. All that if-you-build-it-they-will-come claptrap does not seem to be true for bats. How long did you say it would take? Because it has been six days and I am still batless."

"It can take longer than six days," the clerk said, laughing. "But what can I sell you today?"

"I have a six-inch pipe I need to cover with some kind of mesh," Juna said. "But I need it to be really strong so a rodent, say a ferocious, plague-ridden rat, can't chew through it. Bats I have none, but I seem to have an excess of rats, I swear."

"Are you making a cage out of a pipe?" the clerk asked, puzzled.

"In a manner of speaking," Juna evaded. "Have I come to the right place?"

"Of course you did," Albert answered. "Right this way, Miss Loch."

"Albert has been a great help to me with my projects," Juna said to Hercules as they followed the clerk to the back of the store. "He taught me how to make a bow drill so I can light fires in case I am ever stranded on a desert island. Because you never know. I like to prepared, as I've said before. I like to be useful to my fellow creatures."

"I find you plenty useful," Hercules said to Juna's back.

"Well, what about this?" Albert asked. He was holding up a piece of heavy wire screen.

"That seems acceptable," Juna said, testing it between her fingers. "But how do we attach it? I was thinking a blowtorch, but I don't have a blowtorch. And anyway blowtorches seem a little hazardous."

"A little," Albert agreed. "But here—I can give you a clamp like this one that will cinch around the end of the pipe—you know, the way you hold plastic wrap on a jar with a rubber band. You can tighten it with a screwdriver like this one."

"All right—sold," Juna said. She plunked an unruly pile of crumpled bills on the table.

"Here's your change," Albert said. "But I need to tell you I don't know if this will work. A rat might be able to bite through the wire. I'm not sure. I am not much acquainted with rats, as a friend of mine would say."

"We'll report back on our success," Juna said. "Will I see you this weekend?"

"I hope so—I found a place we can get a lot of shale to make our arrowheads out of."

"What about glass?" Juna suggested. "Can we make them out of glass? I was thinking we might not find the right kind of rock on the desert island, but chances are we'd have some glass from the crash."

"What crash?" Hercules asked, confused.

"Why would I be on a desert island if I didn't crash, I ask

you. I like to be prepared, but I'm not *stupid*." She scooped up the wire screen, the clamp, and the screwdriver. "Can Hercules come, too, to the arrowhead lesson? He's another one who likes to be useful."

"Sure," Albert said. "Of course you're welcome to come, Hercules. Any friend of Juna's is a friend of mine. How about Saturday morning?"

"Sure," Juna said, heading to the door. "We'll see you Saturday. Come on, Hercster."

Hercules followed Juna docilely out of the store, his spirits sinking. He did not know how to broach the topic of where they would be on Saturday; he had hoped that he and Juna would both be back in the mouse city by then. He fingered the two remaining juminy juminy in his pocket and wondered gloomily how he would convince her to take one. He had to admit he saw no reason why she would join him. Why would she want to leave her dog and her bats, her bow drill and her arrowheads, not to mention her father? He sighed as Juna wheeled to a stop in front of his house.

They went directly to the basement and found the warped door of the darkroom. Even full-sized, Hercules found it unpleasantly dusty and moldering, bathed in the red light. It was very awkward for the two of them to fit under the sink to reach the pipe.

"My strategy here is to work fast," Juna suggested. "Here, this was really *your* idea—you should be the one to save the mice."

Carefully, and a little nervously, Hercules wrapped the wire mesh around the mouth of the pipe and slipped the clamp over it to hold the screen in place. He picked up the screwdriver, but his hands shook as he imagined the pointed face of a rat suddenly appearing on the other side of the mesh.

"My, but you're jumpy," Juna observed. "Can I try?" She edged by him and took the screwdriver, deftly tightening the clamp. "Is that tight enough yet, do you think?"

Each in turn tried to pull the screen free, but it held fast.

"It seems to be holding," Hercules said, sighing with relief. "I think we did it! Quangster will be so pleased! I can't wait to tell him. Let's go right now."

"We can tell him later," Juna said, looking at her watch. "But now it's time for Princess' evening constitutional. Are you up for a walk? Let's go, and then maybe we can talk about dinner."

"But Quangster—" Hercules started. He looked longingly at the hole and pleadingly at Juna's back, but she was already heading out of the basement. He stood for a moment, biting his lip, and then hurried after her toward her house.

"I wish it weren't Tuesday," Juna was saying. "My dad's teaching a late class. I can't wait for you to meet him. He'll be thrilled to hear about *our* day, let me tell you."

"My parents would like to meet you, too," Hercules said under his breath. It was true. He imagined how relieved his parents would be if he went back home. He imagined how his mother would pat him on the shoulder and smile at him proudly before peppering Juna with questions; he was sure she would be grateful that Juna had rescued her son from the world within the walls.

But then again, he didn't *want* to be rescued from within the walls—he wanted to return to his hero's welcome, to be the Mother of the Mice, to live with Quangster as they had lived in the days before the rat threat. And he wanted Juna to be there. They could introduce ice cream to the mice. Maybe they could even rig up some mouse bicycles—micycles, they might call them. . . . Who knew? With Juna, it might be perfect.

When they opened the kitchen door, Princess bounded out to greet them, barking hysterically. "Enough of that," Juna said severely, but her tone was affectionate, and she gave the big dog a squeeze. "I missed you, too, but that's no reason to have a coronary, I swear. This dog," she said to Hercules. "You'd think she thought she'd never see me again. And she's like that when I come back from the bathroom."

"It must be nice to have someone like you that much," Hercules ventured.

"Isn't it?" Juna agreed. "Takes the sting out of the morons, don't you find?"

Juna, Hercules, and Princess walked back out into the cool of the evening. The sun was setting; the pink light in the west was very lovely. Juna was talking happily about how they could fix up the darkroom. She said she had her own camera and they could take pictures and develop them together. She did not know what chemicals to use, she admitted, but she was on very good terms with several of the librarians and thought they could learn all about it. Hercules had never felt so torn. He imagined with pleasure standing beside Juna in the mysterious red light of the darkroom as their photographs appeared on the blank white paper, but then his thoughts strayed into the hole and up through the walls to Quangster and Marla and the rest of the mice. In his confusion, he felt he could barely put one foot in front of the other. He *knew* where he belonged, he told himself; he belonged with the mice. He looked at Juna, still confidently spinning out their future, and the two remaining pieces of juminy juminy felt heavy in his pocket.

"I have to go back to Quangster," he said suddenly.

Juna looked disappointed. "But—" she objected. Then checked herself. "Of course you do," she said. "Go and tell Quangster what we did. I'll still be here when you come back. Maybe I'll see if we can rustle up a bicycle for you. I'll teach you to ride. I'm a very patient teacher, I swear. I—"

Hercules took a deep breath and tried again. "Juna," he said, pressing a piece of juminy juminy in her hand, "won't you take it? It's the last I have, except the one for myself. Come back with me. We'll be safe now in the mouse city, and we'll have a great time there. I know the food isn't perfect," he admitted hurriedly, "but we could come out of the walls for a meal now and then. . . ."

Juna stared at him. "What, me—go back, for good?" She laughed, but her face fell when she realized he was serious. She looked at him closely and then sighed. "Don't you see?" she said. "You know I couldn't go back for good. I don't want to be a mouse, Hercules—I kinda like being a human."

Hercules kicked at the ground. He couldn't think of the right words to say.

"I think you'd like being human, too," added Juna.

"But I can't leave Quangster," Hercules said unhappily. "And I wouldn't be able to understand him even if he *could* visit me. . . . And besides, I have responsibilities. . . . I'm the Steward, the Mother of the Mice. . . ."

"But, Hercules," Juna Loch reproached him softly. "They don't need you anymore. You saved them. The rats are trapped for good. The screen will hold. And even if it doesn't, we can go back and replace it. And you know, Hercules, you couldn't do that if you were small. . . . Besides, you should see the war and pestilence and suffering that need your attention out here. You can find plenty of responsibility Outside the Walls, too, I swear."

Hercules thought of the war and pestilence and suffering, on large and small scales, and compared it to the quiet peace of boating on the lake beside the hydroponic gardens, where the little sunflowers bowed and turned their heads toward the fragrant glow of the cheese-sun.

"But that's my *home*. Quangster—the others—they're like my family. I have to go back. If you won't take this piece of juminy juminy, I'll—I'll just throw it away."

"But, Hercules," Juna pleaded. "Don't you see you can't stay there? Remember what happened with Sangster? I'm sorry to put it this way, but how much longer will Quangster live? And then what will you do? Make a new friend who will grow up a hundred times quicker than you? Stay, Hercules. We can grow up together." She looked at him sadly. "What's there for you that's not here with me?"

Hercules opened his mouth and closed it again without saying the two words on the tip of his tongue.

"I have to go," he said instead.

"All right, then," Juna said gently. She took his hand in her own warm palm and laid the piece of juminy juminy on it. "You use the juminy juminy. Go say good-bye. But save the last piece and come back when you're ready."

"No," said Hercules, shaking his head miserably. "You don't understand. I'm going to go, but not to say good-bye. *This* is the good-bye I have to say, if you won't come back with me."

There was a long silence.

"Well, at least keep the juminy juminy," Hercules said. "Then, if you change your mind—"

"*You* keep it," said Juna. "Keep it as a souvenir, so you don't forget me."

"I couldn't forget you," Hercules said, looking at the ground.

There seemed nothing more to say.

"Well, then," said Juna sadly. "Get along, then."

She turned around and walked back toward her house. When she was halfway there, she turned. "Hey!" she called back to him. "Maybe you can send me letters by pigeon sometime." Then she waved once and turned away.

Hercules felt miserable as he pushed open his front door. Half of him wanted to find his mother, to have her rumple his hair and reassure him. But in the end he slipped quietly into his room. He didn't want to have to explain to her, too, why he was better off living the rest of his life with mice.

NO ONE WAS OUT when Hercules returned to the mouse city. Streamers and confetti littered the empty streets, mixed in with the discarded wrappers of roasted seeds. Ripped bunting hung limply from the buildings. Near the edge of town, Hercules came upon a young couple, just emerging from under the grandstand, who shook him enthusiastically by the hand. "Thank you for the cheese, Steward! Such a celebration will be remembered for *lak* generations!" they shouted, before running off and leaving Hercules alone again.

"You don't know the half of it—" Hercules began, but they were too far away. "Of course not—you didn't even know you were in danger in the first place."

"Don't be too hard on your children, Steward He-Who-Counts-Past-*lak*," came a voice behind him. It was so like Sangster's that he turned around in a flash, hoping, wishing—but it was Marla. "We have all been blind and hairless, Steward, but soon it will be time for us to see. But come, I have been sent to watch for you. Quangster will be relieved you have returned in time." She looked around with concern. "Where is the other human? Is she—"

"She's fine," Hercules said. "She just wouldn't come back with me. But we have bought you more time—maybe time for *lak lak* generations." And he told her of how they had sealed the pipe.

"How wonderful!" she exclaimed, clapping her paws together. "We should set the song-wrights to composing ballads in your honor this very moment. You may have given us all the time we need, not only for *lak lak* generations, but for all generations. Quangster has found a permanent solution. Oh, Steward Small Ears! Today will be the beginning of a great era for mice—all mice will learn to read, and all mice will learn to count. We will grow. Not in height, of course, but in goodness and in wisdom."

Hercules couldn't tell why he didn't feel elated at this news. Faces swam before his eyes: Sangster's, his parents', Quangster's, and Juna Loch's; he felt as unhappy as he had when he'd seen Sangster's body lying on her deathbed.

They found Quangster in the Steward's chambers. He was writing something on a scroll with a look of intense concentration on his face.

"Quangster, the Steward has returned," Marla announced as they entered the room. "He and his friend have bought us time. They have trapped the rats in their pipe."

Quangster ran to Hercules and embraced him. "Small Ears!" he cried out in relief. "I hoped you would return before—"

"Before the rats came?" Hercules interrupted. "But, Quangster! Juna Loch and I have caged the rats in their pipe. They will not be able to escape for some time yet. There is time to breathe, time to relax. . . ."

"Oh, Small Ears! Once more you have given us—given me—what we need! I thank you, Small Ears, on my behalf and on behalf of all mice. And I am so glad—so relieved—that you have arrived before I go to see Kitty Joas for the last time. I have decided on my favor. I just pray she will not deny me."

"What will you ask?"

"I will ask her to take this city out of time, as her lands are out of time. It will make us permanently invisible to ants and rats. The ants can tunnel right through our city, and we will be safe forever."

"Isn't it wonderful?" Marla asked Hercules, taking Quangster by the arm with a proprietary look of pride. "You have given us the time for Quangster to save us for good."

"I—I don't know what to say," Hercules said honestly.

"I was ready to call for Kitty Joas just as you came," Quangster said. "But now that you bring us your good news, we have time for a talk before we go. Tell me of your adventures. Tell me how you trapped the rats in the pipe."

So Hercules recounted his adventures in great detail, from the capture by the ants to Juna's freeing of the fireflies ("She is noble!" Quangster cried. "What a worthy creature to be your friend!") to the slimy trip into the rat stronghold. Quangster and Marla were very quiet as Hercules described the enemy.

"I am glad we did not choose to fight them," Marla said. "I would not like to experience hate the way those rats hate us. I do not want to believe that might makes right."

"And what was it like?" Quangster asked. "What was it like, among the Feet?"

Hercules paused in his narration. He did not know how to answer. "I liked it very much," he said slowly. "When I was there, I mean, I liked it very much—not as much as I like it here, of course, but. . . . It is very bright outside. The colors are more beautiful, the smells are better, and I had ice cream. And Juna Loch. . . ."

But he did not know how to finish that sentence. He felt as if the closet shelves on which his emotions had been neatly piled had suddenly broken and all his feelings were left in a jumbled mess he could not face sorting out.

"It sounds like a wonderful place for you to live," Quangster said gently. "I am glad."

"I'm not going to live there," Hercules began. "I've come back to stay with you and Marla forever—"

Quangster held up his paw. "Time passes," he said. "And Small Ears, much as I want to talk with you, I am anxious for Kitty Joas' answer." He turned to Marla. "I do not know if she will open her gates to you, as well, Marla. If not, I have said to you all I have words to say. I believe you know my mind, and I know you know my heart." His voice was more choked and tender than Hercules had ever heard before.

Quangster walked to the middle of the room and stood with his paws pressed together. "Kitty Joas, Kitty Joas," he called, and the walls melted away at once. Marla's mouth fell open as she slowly turned in a circle, taking in the leafy statues, the glass palace, the bright sky. Then the Tugot's voice rang out, as clear and as painfully cold as a mountain stream.

"Well come, my child Marla. Well come also, my child

Quangster. And you, Hercules Amsterdam. Well, Quangster, are you ready to ask your favor of me?"

"My lady," Quangster began, quietly but evenly, "in your wisdom you live out of time here in your glorious palace. My favor is that you choose another time, not the present and not your future, in which our city can exist unmolested. I beg that you make it as invisible to the rats as the glories of this palace are invisible to all within the walls."

"I have always admired you for grasping such a wise idea," Kitty Joas replied. "Even Ulrich would not have come up with so elegant a solution."

"Can you do it?" Quangster asked.

"I can do it now," Kitty Joas answered, "but first, you understand that I always expect my children to give something in return for my favors?"

"I do," Quangster said. "I have been thinking of it since the first moment we met." Marla's paw curled around Quangster's and squeezed it tightly, but Quangster did not react. He seemed more serene than Hercules had ever seen him. "I am ready now," he said, "but I have some words for my friend." And he motioned toward Hercules.

"Then I accept," Kitty Joas said, waving her arms expansively. "I will give you a moment, and then it will be as you wished. The city will be hidden forever to all but mouse eyes. If you must speak to this human, this is the time. I will go and converse with my daughter Marla. When I return, it will be done." Slowly, as if in a trance, Marla followed the Tugot, leaving Hercules and Quangster alone.

Hercules stared at his friend.

"What just happened?" he asked.

"It's over," Quangster replied. "You heard her. We are safe." He sounded very tired. For the first time Hercules noticed how gray Quangster had become. He was a true silverback now. If he had been a human, he would have been a man past middle age, and Hercules was still a boy of ten.

"Please don't look so unhappy, Small Ears," Quangster begged. "Today is a day for rejoicing. We are safe, safe forever. This is a day of great transformation for all of us. Today the Black Chronicle should be re-covered in white. All mice should hear what is within." He paused and looked tenderly at Hercules.

"Today is a day of great change for you as well, Small Ears," he went on. "Now it is time to lay down your burden. The secret of the Stewards will be secret no longer. No longer will it need to weigh upon you. You have done your duty, Small Ears. It is time to for you to breathe freely. And," he added softly, "perhaps it is time for you to leave. All mice will understand that there are other pulls on your affection now."

"No!" Hercules cried. "No, Quangster, I'm not going to leave you—" He choked, then, and looked up to his friend for help. Quangster's brown eyes were deep and kind as they looked down on Hercules. Hercules stared back at Quangster for a long while, and then he found the words he could not say to Juna Loch.

"I'm scared," he said.

Quangster's wise eyes shone, and he took Hercules' hand between his two paws. "I know," he answered.

He stepped back then. Marla and Kitty Joas were returning.

"There is not much time," Quangster said calmly, looking Hercules full in the face. "The last thing I have to say is this: I have always loved you as a brother, Small Ears. The great honor of my life has been to know you as a friend."

He moved away from Hercules and joined his paw to Marla's. Then, in a strong voice, he called out, "Kitty Joas, I am ready." The glass castle, the mountains, all the topiary disappeared; they were back in the familiarity of the Steward's chambers. And Quangster fell dead to the ground.

18

QUANGSTER'S GRAY AND BROWN BODY lay still at Hercules' feet.

"What?" screamed Hercules. Marla bowed her head. "Quangster! What happened? Are you all right?"

Marla laid her paw on his arm. "Don't you see, Uncle?" she whispered. "He is dead. Shouting will not bring him back."

"Dead?" Hercules cried. "Why is he dead? Is *this* what he promised Kitty Joas?" He flailed his arms in impotent rage and kicked at a chair. Tears sprang from his eyes.

"Quangster knew what he was doing, Uncle," Marla soothed. She knelt down and stroked the coarse fur of Quangster's brow with a look of such loving admiration that it made Hercules even wilder with grief.

"How can you just *accept* it?" he shouted. Then, embarrassed to be disturbing the stillness with so much noise, he started over, quietly, miserably. "Didn't you—didn't you love him?"

"Of course I loved him," she answered, bending down and kissing the closed eyes. "In another time, perhaps, we would have married. But after all, a mouse's life is not worth much. . . ."

"It was to *me*," Hercules said bitterly. He crouched down beside Quangster's body. In death, the sweet face looked more noble than ever. "Quangster," he choked, tentatively touching his friend. "Please, Quangster, don't be dead."

They sat silently by Quangster's body for a long time. Then Hercules looked to Marla. "I don't understand how he could do this to us," he said.

"He didn't do it *to* us, Small Ears," said Marla maternally. "He did it *for* us, for all of us. He sacrificed himself for what he loved most."

A painful tangle of emotions twisted tighter within Hercules—rage and anguish and the desperate feeling of his own inadequacy. "I—maybe *I* should have been the one to do it. I was the Steward, but I never could do that—he was so brave—"

"It should not have been you," said Marla, patting Hercules' hand. "You are the Steward, of course, but you are also a child. And this is not truly your world, Small Ears. And when your time comes, you will be able to make the sacrifices you need to make."

"This *is* my world," he protested. Marla watched him patiently, saying nothing. Her eyes reminded him of Sangster's when, so long ago, she had suggested he return to the world Outside the Walls. "Why do you look at me like that? I do belong here! I belong here with you! We'll found the school—

teach the mice to read—we'll teach them all about Quangster, you and I."

"I can do those things without you," Marla answered quietly. She folded her hands and waited; she looked more like Sangster than ever.

"I can't go," Hercules whispered. "I'm not ready. . . ."

Marla bent over Quangster's head once more and murmured, "You know, we lie to the young when we say it is the golden time of life. I think it is harder to be a child than anything else."

Hercules went to the window. He threw open the iron shutters and let the bright cheese light come flooding in. He stared out at the quiet mouse city, the laundry flapping on the line, and listened to the sounds of friendly mouse banter that wafted up from the lower levels. In the distance, he could hear the cheers from the bleachers next to the baseball diamond. It was all so peaceful.

"What can I do, Marla?" he whispered finally. "If I go, I can never come back—I can't do it."

"You may feel you *can't* go," she said, as patient as ever. "But do you *want* to go?"

"I don't know," he said, looking down at Quangster.

"There is another thing, Small Ears," Marla said. "When I was walking with Kitty Joas, she gave me something for you." She handed Hercules a folded paper. There was a single sentence only, written in English: *The Plague Rat is searching for you and Juna Loch.*

Hercules twisted the paper in his hands. "How can I—" he whispered, and then he looked down at Quangster's body and understood what he had to do. "I have to go," he said. "Goodbye, Marla. Tell the mice—" But he didn't have time to finish the sentence. He was already down the stairs and racing out of the library, leaving Marla and Quangster behind him.

"Hold on, Juna," he said to himself as he ran down the pathway past the dump. He sped down the little streets that turned to broad avenues and finally back to the downward-sloping boulevard that led to the baseball field. To his left ran the little passage of the cheese-gatherers, the passage that led out of the walls. He took a breath and climbed the ladder. Steeling himself, as a person does when about to jump into frigid water, he took a deep breath and a running jump into the passageway.

When he looked back, it was all gone. The warm sun of the cheese lamp, the baseball diamond, Marla, Quangster, the houses in the distance—they were all subsumed in blackness. He retraced his steps, hands out to feel the invisible city, but it was more than invisible. It was as if it were not there. Even the sounds of the mouse city had been silenced; all he heard was the rush of water in the pipes and the occasional creak of old timbers. But there was no time for misery; at any moment the Plague Rat could be at Juna's throat. *Come on,* he said to himself determinedly.

At that moment, the ants burst through the wall.

"The Feet!" one shouted. Hercules was instantly surrounded by large black trackers who ran the length of the corridor, wagging their antennae into every corner.

"Enemy," said the ant who had spoken first, "I am the princess Formoise. I command this squadron of workers for the Mother-Highness. You are the Escaped One. It will be my great honor to return you to the dairy once we have located the mouse city."

"You'll never be able to find it," Hercules said, proud and

sad all at the same time. "Kitty Joas has hidden it so it will never be found. The mice have been saved for eternity."

Several trackers returned to Formoise. "This is strange, Sister-Princess-Captain," one said. "The smell of mice is heavy here, and yet there is nothing. The scent seems simply to end."

"What trick is this?" Formoise asked Hercules.

"I told you," Hercules repeated. "The Tugot has hidden them forever. Now get out of my way. I have urgent business."

"We'll see about that," said Formoise. "Sisters!" she called out, and Hercules had the sinking feeling he had not played his cards exactly right. "We return to our Mother-Highness for instructions!" And three ants lifted Hercules into the air as if he were no more cumbersome than a canoe carried by a trio of humans.

At first he struggled, but the ants nipped at him with their sharp mandibles. Instead he tried hard to send Juna psychic messages. *Unajay!* he called to her in his head. *Ebay arefulcay!* Then, hopefully, he noticed that the blackness around him was growing gray and grainy, and the smell of the sewer was growing stronger, too. They were drawing near the hole into the darkroom; they were drawing near his point of escape.

"Yes," said Formoise, "here we are back at the scene of your crime, the site where you sought to trick our allies. You thought you were clever, but, like a lazy drone, you didn't finish the job. With our assistance, the rats will soon escape. Our mother does not forget her friends. Sisters!" she commanded. "Put him down! Let him face his enemy!"

The ants dropped Hercules in front of the pipe. Three rats clung by their claws to the mesh, busily gnawing at the wires. The screen was silver with little tooth marks, and a few wires were already broken. One of the rats stopped his work and stared at Hercules with hatred. "Human," he growled, in a voice thick with slobber, "you thought you had trapped us, but we will not be caged. You should have had the courage to face us in battle."

"We didn't want to sink to your level," said Hercules. "We will not be rats. We did not need to shed a drop of your blood to rescue the mice—we needed only to delay you until Kitty Joas could save them. It was the poetical way."

The rat looked at him in confusion, and then, somewhat less forcefully, went on, "The Plague Rat will find you, you miserable worm. And when he is sure that you are dead, he will return to share his weapons with us all, and the Legs will fall before us. When we escape this pitiful prison, your family will be first, you cowering girl! See your shoddy handiwork! It was the work of a female. Already we have bitten through two bars. . . ."

A sudden idea, a poetical idea, flitted through Hercules' brain, and a wide smile spread over his face.

"What are you smiling at, you female!" the rat snarled.

"You may be warriors," Hercules said, trying to keep from laughing, "but you were so easily caged—and by a female at that. For all your strength and might making right, you were done in by a female."

"You should have stood and fought like a male!" the rat growled. The ants behind Hercules began to buzz with indignation, but the rat went on obliviously. "Are all humans so femalish? No wonder you fall in Black Death before us! This cage was a useless gesture, the weak gesture of a woman! Why did you trust anything to that female? Are you not the male, the brains, the muscle, and the will?"

The buzzing and clicking of the ants grew even louder behind Hercules, and he smiled wider than ever as he felt rough feet push him aside. Formoise stepped forward to address the largest of the rats.

"Perhaps I did not hear you correctly," she said, speaking slowly to the rats, as though they were very stupid. "Weak? Females are *weak?*"

"Weak as water," the rat said, and spit. And then Hercules laughed with pleasure and relief.

Suddenly, Formoise shouted out something in a voice so high that Hercules could not hear it. Within moments, ants were appearing out of nowhere with boards and wooden pegs. They began to erect a wooden structure over the pipe as quickly as if it had been conjured up by Kitty Joas herself.

"Weak as water?" Formoise repeated disdainfully to the rats, who stared at her in sullen confusion. "The ancient contract ends here, you useless drones. My mother will sever all relations with rats when she hears of your insults to her and all our sisters. She will station a guard to watch this place, to keep the cage in good repair. You will no longer set foot in her dominions." Two ants carrying a board pushed Hercules brusquely out of the way. They pressed the board firmly over the rat's surprised face, catching his whiskers. Hercules backed away toward the wall of the tunnel. The ants, under Formoise's direction, continued adding layer upon layer to the wooden prison. They did not see Hercules as he rushed toward the hole to the darkroom.

He paused at the door before he ran into the world Outside the Walls, and looked back toward the rat pipe. It was covered with ants, clicking and waving their antennae in fury. He wished he could tell Quangster. Then he felt a sharp stab of sadness, not because he had not remembered that Quangster was dead, but because he had remembered it so quickly. "I hate it!" he said. The piece of juminy juminy was cold in his hand. "Kitty Joas!" he whispered angrily. "Listen to me! I am taking the last piece. But Quangster should not be dead. Bring him back and I will never enter the walls again." There was no response. Taking a deep breath and one backward glance, Hercules stepped through the hole. As he left the world within the walls, he thought for a flicker of a moment that the tunnel had shimmered with green and light, as if Kitty Joas had partially opened her gates in answer, but he could not be sure he had not imagined it.

What he did not imagine, however, were the marks of feet—clawed feet—rat's feet—leading across the dusty darkroom floor into the basement. Hercules' heart leaped into his throat. He imagined the rat tracking Juna's scent along the path that led to her house—it was as if they had laid down a red carpet for it to follow. He fumbled in his pocket for the juminy juminy and almost dropped it in his hurry. And then he swallowed it.

He began following the Plague Rat's tracks even as he grew. By the time he had reached full size, he was already at the front door of his house. He ran down the street toward Juna's. Two of the boys were in front of the house next door. They yelled something at Hercules, but he waved an impatient hand at them. His mind was racing faster than his feet, wondering how he could defeat the Plague Rat. What did a rat fear? Only the enemy with the name too terrible to mention. That was not a person, but a person was its master. But before he could figure it out, he had arrived at Juna's house and burst through the unlocked front door. There was Juna on the couch, apparently asleep, and a small shadow near her head made Hercules freeze. On the other side of the latched kitchen door, Princess barked angrily at the sound of an intruder. Shuddering, Hercules remembered how long Princess' teeth had seemed when she had bared them at the squirrel on Juna's lawn—and suddenly Hercules knew what to do.

"Juna!" he cried. "Get up on the back of the couch! I figured it out—the rats' worst enemies are dogs!" And then (steeling himself for the teeth and claws of the German shepherd) he lifted the latch on the kitchen door.

In a flash, everything twisted into motion: the rat leaped at Juna; Juna leaped toward Princess; and Princess—so fast she seemed to turn to liquid—swept across the room and then out the open front door with the rat dangling from her jaws.

"Holy Moly," Juna said, staring after the swinging door, which still flapped in Princess' wake. "Holy Moly, that's all I can say. Holy of Holiest Moly."

"But you're okay?" Hercules asked, worried.

Juna inspected her arms and legs. "I seem to have the full complement of limbs," she concluded, "and they seem to be free from rat bites and scratches. Yes, I believe I'm fine. But you, Hercules! You seem large."

"I'm back," he said simply.

"Yes, I observe you are back, Hercules Amsterdam. I cannot express to you how glad I am that you are back, and I am mightily glad not to be infected by that rat. I have read about the bubonic plague, and it's not my preferred death, let me tell you. It involves something called a bubo, and I prefer not to be killed by something with so embarrassing a name. I am also grateful not to have my nose eaten off. It's not a very good nose, but it is the only one I have. And besides, it was given to me by my mother before she skipped. But, Hercules—thank you for coming to save me. I am more grateful than I can say." She awkwardly opened her arms to him. They hugged, and then Hercules wriggled free, embarrassed.

"Juna," he said, "Kitty Joas killed Quangster."

"Oh, Hercules," Juna said mournfully. "I'm so sorry."

She reached out and put a sympathetic hand on his shoulder. He was glad to be standing next to her, but the warmth of her hand made him miss Quangster even more. He thought of how Quangster used to tag after him and call him Uncle, and of the trip they took together to the Box while Quangster quaked beside him. Then he remembered Quangster's amazing feat of reading every book in the library and their discovery of the existence of Kitty Joas; he thought of how Quangster had grown so calm in the face of danger. Hercules had witnessed it all. In his final moments, Quangster had called Hercules his brother, but (Hercules thought with a pang) Quangster had become the elder brother, almost an uncle. He had sent Hercules off with confidence and love, knowing he would never see Hercules grow.

"He would have been proud of you," Juna said. "It took courage to do what you did, Hercules. You stepped right up to the plate and took the bull by the horns. *You* should be proud of you, Herco."

Hercules said nothing.

"Anyhoo," Juna said, fishing for the belt out of the closet and buckling it around her waist. "There's plenty of work to do. First order of business: let's make certain those plague-ridden fleas have not taken up residence on our good friend Princess. A trip to the vet is probably in order. I suppose we ought to call the Department of Health or the CDC or the NIH or the

ASPCA or something. And then let's go save another civilization. Let's do it in Quangster's name, what say you? But first,
dinner. Have you eaten? As I have remarked before, saving civilization is hungry work. How does canned soup sound? Or do
you only eat cereral? I went through a period when I only ate
cereal, and that's the truth. But it's very fortified. I was so fortified I was like a battleship, I swear. . . ."

Hercules gave a small smile. As he was following Juna into
the kitchen, he noticed a little sugar ant scurrying across the
floor. He was about to step on it when he stopped himself.

"I won't be a rat," he whispered, and then Hercules Amsterdam, fifty-one inches tall, stepped over the threshold into
his new life.

IF HERCULES HAD KNOWN a little more about math, it would have been easier to teach Quangster to count past three. If he had known how the ancient Greeks or Israelites wrote numbers—assigning letters of the alphabet to each number— that might have been enough. What really would have helped him, however, would have been an understanding of the different base systems for counting. What he needed was this appendix.

Most humans, no matter what names they give to the numbers, count in a similar way. Instead of giving a completely unique name to each of the infinite numbers, they have names for a small number of them. They then use those names in combination to name the rest. In English, the unique numbers are: zero, one, two, three, four, five, six, seven, eight, nine, ten, hundred, thousand, and million. All the other numbers[1] are combinations of those first ten (twenty = two tens; thirty = three tens, etc.). The really big numbers—billion, trillion, quadrillion, and so on—combine the Greek names for two, three, four, and so on, with the ending *illion* to make it sound like a million—the Italian word for *big thousand*.

Our way of counting is based on the first ten numbers, and that is why we call it a base ten system. There is nothing particularly special about the number ten, you understand, except the fact that most humans have ten fingers, which makes counting in base ten particularly easy. It's not the only way to count—some ancient human cultures actually used base twelve or even base sixty. There are still some remnants of those base systems in our lives (the way we tell time, for example, or measure the 360 degrees of a circle).

It's easiest to see the special role ten plays in the base ten system when we write the numbers in symbols rather than in words. We write each of the infinite numbers by combining just ten symbols (0, 1, 2, 3, 4, 5, 6, 7, 8, 9) in different ways. Instead of coming up with a new symbol for numbers bigger than nine, we simply make a new column that counts how many tens we have next to the column that counts the ones. The numeral 10, then, counts how many tens (one) and how many ones (zero). The number 11 counts how many tens (one) and how many ones (one). The number 33 counts how many tens (three: three tens = thirty) and how many ones (three), and so on.

---

[1]Eleven and twelve might seem an exception to this rule, but they aren't. In Old English, *eleven* means "one left over" and *twelve* "two left over"—that is, one and two left over ten.

Once we get more than nine tens, we don't make a new symbol for one hundred (i.e., ten tens), but simply add another column to count the hundreds. Once we get more than ten hundreds, rather than make a new symbol for one thousand, we add a new column to count the thousands. And so on.

This way of writing numbers may seem obvious, but it is relatively recent. It was invented in India and brought to Europe in the Middle Ages by Arabs, which is why those numerals are called Arabic numbers. Before Arabic numerals became widespread, people had more cumbersome systems. The Hebrews and the Greeks gave letters of the alphabet to the lower numbers (so, for the Greeks, 1 = alpha, 2 = beta, 3 = gamma, etc.). The Romans had a system (now mostly relegated to clock faces) where I = 1, V = 5, X = ten, and L = 50.[2] Arabic numbers have a huge advantage over the Greek and Roman systems. See how easy it is to do the following problem:

$$123$$
$$+\ 24$$

You simply add the ones column $(3 + 4 = 7)$, then the tens column $(2 + 2 = 4)$, then the hundreds column $(1 + 0 = 1)$, and come up with 147: simplicity itself. In contrast, the poor Romans had no easy-to-add columns. If they wanted to add:

[2]Like the mice, the Greeks, Romans, and Hebrews stopped counting at some point and just used a word that meant "large number" (analogous to our unofficial word *kazillion*). Their large numbers were much smaller than a kazillion. The word *myriad*—which we, like the Greeks, use to mean "a lot"—was only a thousand.

they would have had to use an abacuslike counting board or count on their fingers to find the answer of CXLVII.

Hercules might have saved Quangster some confusion by acting like the Greeks or the Hebrews and just assigning letters of the tailscript alphabet to the first seven numbers, since the idea was only to show his friend that there can be names for numbers higher than three. The crude way he taught Quangster, however, could end up being helpful to mice, since it would eventually allow them to use just four digits (0, 1, 2, 3) to write each of the infinite numbers, rather than limiting them to the number of letters in the alphabet. While it may seem amazing that just four digits can express as many numbers as ten digits can, it is perfectly possible, as you can see below.

Although he didn't know it, what Hercules was trying to do was teach Quangster the base-four system (called base four because it's based on only those four digits mentioned above: 0, 1, 2, and 3). He didn't do it exactly right because he forgot about the existence of zero, but this is forgivable. Even the most brilliant Greeks and Romans didn't understand the concept of zero, and Hercules was only a boy of ten without benefit of this appendix.

The base-four system uses the same principles as base ten. You count up to three in the ones column, and then (instead of coming up with a new symbol for four) make a new column that counts how many fours you have. Remember how this works in our base-ten system, where each column is a different multiple of ten:

$$1 , 0\ 0\ 0 , 0\ 0\ 0$$

- $10 \times 10 \times 10 \times 10 \times 10 \times 10 = $ millions
- $10 \times 10 \times 10 \times 10 \times 10 = $ hundred-thousands
- $10 \times 10 \times 10 \times 10 = $ ten-thousands
- $10 \times 10 \times 10 = $ thousands
- $10 \times 10 = $ hundreds
- tens
- ones

The same holds true with the base-four system, where each column is a multiple of four:

$$1 , 0\ 0\ 0 , 0\ 0\ 0$$

- $4 \times 4 \times 4 \times 4 \times 4 \times 4 = 4{,}096$s
- $4 \times 4 \times 4 \times 4 \times 4 = 1{,}024$s
- $4 \times 4 \times 4 \times 4 = 256$s
- $4 \times 4 \times 4 = 64$s
- $4 \times 4 = 16$s
- fours
- ones

But here's where you need to hold on to your hat. In base four, the number written as "10" is not the number ten. The numeral to the left counts not how many tens you have, but how many fours: in this case, one. In base four, the number written "10" is actually the number four. I swear.

Similarly, in base four, the number "11" is not the number eleven. It has a one in the fours column, and a one in the ones column: four + one = five.

"33" has three in the fours column (three × four = twelve) and a three in the ones column: twelve + three = fifteen.

The number "123" has a one in the sixteens column, two in the fours column (eight), and three in the ones column: sixteen + eight + three = twenty-seven.

How do you figure out how to write numbers in base four? Let's take forty-two as an example. We know that there won't be anything in the sixty-four column, since forty-two is less than sixty-four no matter how you count. But we can put a "2" in the sixteen column (two sixteens are thirty-two). Subtracting this thirty-two from the original number, we get ten left over. We can think of that ten as eight plus two, and put a "2" in the four column (two fours = eight), leaving a "2" for the ones column. In base four, then, forty-two is written "222": (two × sixteen) + (two × four) + two.

Try it now yourself. How do you write twenty-three in base four? What number does "23" represent in base four? (The answers follow at the end of the appendix.)

An Appendix to the Appendix

While most people living today use the base-ten system, we are surrounded by another way of counting: the base two, or binary, system, which has only two digits: 0 and 1. This is the preferred base system of computer programming, since computers can use little OFF and ON switches to correspond to the ones and zeros in order to store information electronically. Many computer languages use ones and zeros to represent numbers, and those numbers can represent any letter or symbol on a computer keyboard.

How do you write big numbers (or even small ones) in binary? As with the other base systems, the column farthest to the right represents the number of ones. The next column represents the numbers of twos, the next the number of 2 × 2s, the next the number of 2 × 2 × 2s (just as the thousands column in base ten is 10 × 10 × 10), and so forth. Small numbers require a lot of digits in binary language, but with space, you can write any number you want:

1 = one
10 = one in the twos column and zero in the ones column = two + zero = two
10101010 = one in the one hundred twenty-eight column, zero in the sixty-four column, one in the thirty-two column, zero in the sixteen column, one in the eight column, zero in the four column, one in the two column, and zero in the one column = one hundred twenty-eight + thirty-two + eight + two = one hundred and seventy

An Appendix to the Appendix of the Appendix

It is also possible to use Arabic numbers to represent base systems higher than ten. Some aspects of computer programming use the hexadecimal system, which is base sixteen (hex = six, dec = ten in Greek). Of course, since we only have shapes for the digits 0 through 9, we need some help to write the higher numbers. In hexadecimal, then, the numbers one through fifteen are written: 1, 2, 3, 4, 5, 6, 7, 8, 9, A, B, C, D, E, F (where A = ten, B = eleven, C = twelve, D = thirteen, etc.). You can probably guess, then, that the number sixteen is written "10" (one in the sixteens column, zero in the ones column). If you wanted to write the number twenty-nine in hexadecimal, you'd first take out the sixteen and put a one in the sixteens column, leaving thirteen ("D") in the ones column: 1D. Thirty-four would be written "22" (two in the sixteens column and two in the ones column) and so on. Try it out yourself. The next time you have insomnia, try figuring out what your age is in hexadecimals, or if that's too easy, the year or your phone number. It can't hurt. If you succeed, you will have stretched your brain a little further and learned something that could be useful someday; it not, it will probably put you to sleep.

Answers:
Twenty-three is written "113" in base four (16 + 4 + 3).
"23" in base four is (4 × 2) + 3 = eleven.